ETHELINDE;

OR,

THE FATAL VOW.

A ROMANCE,

BY THE AUTHOR OF "ELA, THE OUTCAST;" "GIPSY BOY;" "EVELINA;" "GALLANT TOM;" &C., &C.

" Absolve me from that vow,
That fatal vow, which holds
A withering curse o'er all my actions."—ORESTES.

LONDON:

PRINTED BY E. LLOYD, 12, SALISBURY SQUARE, FLEET STREET;
PUBLISHED BY G. PURKESS, COMPTON STREET, SOHO.

PREFACE.

IN the present little simple narrative the object of the Author has not been so much to excite mere melodramatic effect, by striking or startling incidents, as to establish a moral by shewing the fatal consequences that invariably ensue from a deviation from the strict path of honour and rectitude, and the complicated evils that follow in the train of a single error.

Unfortunately there are too many designing Mr. Welfords in the world, and it behoves every youthful individual, who may have fortune at command, to be careful that they are not caught in their snares, and by committing themselves in the way in which Major Clarence did, place themselves almost irrecoverably in their power, involving not only their own peace of mind, but the happiness of all that is dearest to them on earth.

Ethelinde Clarence was a damsel of strong mind, of the strictest virtue, and firmly faithful to her first and only love, and thus was she enabled to support the many severe trials to which it was the will of Providence to subject her, and ultimately defeating the plans of her enemies, to meet with her just reward in becoming the happy wife of the man of her choice. In the character of Norman Rayborne, too, the author has endeavoured to shew that although innumerable difficulties may at times present themselves, the man who pursues a career of honour is sure to be able to surmount them, and to look back upon the past with feelings of satisfaction rather than regret.

These objects the author of " ETHELINDE," trusts he has been able to accomplish to the satisfaction and amusement of his readers, and thanking them most cordially for the favour they have bestowed upon his labours, he begs leave to subscribe himself

THEIR OBEDIENT SERVANT.

London, February, 1848.

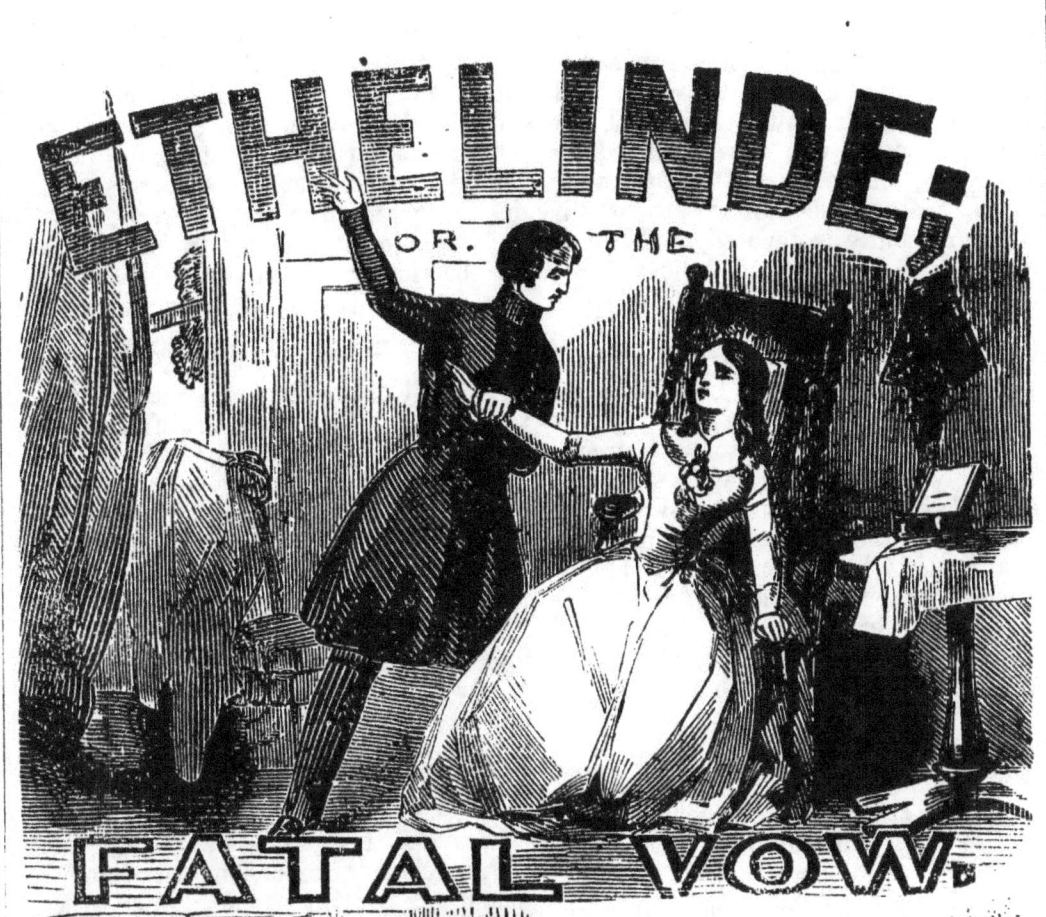

ETHELINDE; OR THE FATAL VOW.

CHAPTER I.

FATHER AND DAUGHTER.—THE TRIAL OF THE HEART.—THE ASSIGNATION, AND ITS CONSEQUENCES.

"I IMPLORE you, dearest father, do not urge me to make any such a promise, which is in direct opposition to my own feelings and sentiments; and which it would require but little self-persuasion to violate—do not urge me to make a vow which must be opposed to my feelings and my principles. Dear father, you have ever found me studious to obey your every wish; ready to fulfil it to the best of my capacity, but in this instance, indeed I cannot, without sacrificing all my earthly hopes,—without suffering a blight to fall upon all my youthful prospects;—such a blight that future days, even had they had all the brightness of my own anticipations—could not recompense. You who have ever been so kind, so indulgent to me, will rather forego your own desires than enforce a proceeding that must render me wretched for ever. Had my sainted mother been living, how strongly, I am convinced, would she have pleaded to you for me ; that mother, that fond, that revered, that gentle mother, to whom your whole soul was devoted, and whose every wish you anticipated, whose every thought blended with your own, and from whom to have dissented would have rendered you miserable for ever. Urge me not then, dearest father, I once more beseech you, not to resign my fate into the hands of one who can at most scarcely possess my esteem. Father, I have no heart to bestow upon Everard Welford."

Such was the earnest, the pathetic appeal made to her parent by Ethelinde Clarence ; the crystal drops first trembling in her brilliant eyes, and then streaming down her beauteous cheeks, as they were seated together in the parlour of their mansion, in the summer of the year 1834.

Melodious was the voice that gave utterance to the words, and heavenly the graces of the fair being from whom they emanated.

To gaze upon that innocent and beauteous countenance ; to contemplate the simple and artless demeanour of that angelic being, and imagine that one impure thought could ever have entered her bosom, would be to libel the Almighty for one of the most lovely of His creations.

Reader, we will not enter into a lengthy, and probably tedious description of the beauties both of mind and person of Ethelinde Clarence, as they will be fully developed in the course of the stirring incidents which will be brought forward on the stage of our narrative.

Her father was a tall, portly, and still handsome man, about fifty years of age. His countenance was generally placid and benevolent, and yet there was at times, an expression in his eyes which bespoke a sort of obstinate determination, and detracted very much from the general contour of his features.

Major Clarence was a man who, generally possessing an amiable mind, had also his weak points, and it was those which came in juxta-position with the feelings and wishes of his lovely daughter in the present instance. Yet when he looked in the agitated countenance of his only child, and saw the pure reflection of a wife he had while living so loved, and whose memory, since it had pleased Heaven to call her to itself, was still so deeply enshrined in his " heart of hearts," he was almost inclined to break down the barrier to his natural inclinations, and rescind the fatal vow which one act of error had, unfortunately, extorted from him.

It would have formed a beautiful subject for the pencil of the skilful artist to have had the opportunity of sketching the father and his lovely daughter, with all the powerful and extraordinary passions of their souls wrought out so prominently on their countenances, at the moment of which we are writing. The one so amiable, but so inflexible upon the point to which he was unfortunately fettered, yet so moved by the appeal of the child he adored, as to be half disposed to shake off, to cast away those shackles ; the other so lovely, so gentle, so supplicating, so eloquently earnest in the suit she so simply and so innocently urged, and in which the whole of her future hopes, her prospects, her happiness were probably involved.

Poor Ethelinde !—there were, indeed, dark days, many months of misery and severe trial in store for you. The demon of torture had marked you for its victim, and too soon were you destined to experience its power.

It was an elegant and spacious apartment, that in which Major Clarence and our heroine were seated. They were near the window, which descended to the ground, and was open, it being a beautiful evening in the month of July ; and from that window was commanded one of the most lovely and diversified prospects in that " garden of England," the county of Kent. Sweet and refreshing came the breeze, redolent with the last sweet perfume of closing flowers, and which served to revive the almost crushed spirits of Ethelinde. Everything was calm and beautiful on the face of nature. Nature luxuriated in one of her most beautiful moods ! Who, that ever possessed a thought, one ennobling feeling, would have gazed upon that scene, and at such a season, without wondering at, admiring, and revering the Great, the Almighty Ruler of all?

The monarch of the day had nearly performed his course, and his golden beams were fast retiring from the enraptured gaze in one bright molten sheet of glory, behind the western hills, shedding a soft and tranquil halo upon every surrounding object as he departed.

Oh, who could entertain one idea but that of reverence and delight, who gazed and *thought!*

A long pause ensued after the tender appeal made by Ethelinde Clarence, which we have recorded at the commencement of our tale. How earnestly did the fair girl's eyes plead to her father's heart; those eyes, which were the index to one of the most pure of souls.

And could her father meet that gaze unmoved? Oh, no!—he took her tiny hand within his; he imprinted a kiss upon her snowy forehead—for several minutes he could not speak, but the convulsive agitation of his countenance, and the heavings of his chest, plainly showed the powerful and torturing emotions which were struggling in his bosom, and to which he could not give utterance.

Several efforts did he make to speak, but he failed, and at length gently resigning his daughter's hand, he abruptly arose from his seat, and traversed the apartment in a disordered manner. Our heroine remained in the same attitude, but never moved from her chair, or took her earnest gaze from her father. It was one of the most painful moments she had ever experienced. How agonizing were the feelings which were struggling at her heart!—Filial duty urged her one way, but, if possible, even a more tender sentiment contended against it, and thoughts which will shortly be more fully explained, tempted her, at all hazards, to risk the importunities of her father.

At length he advanced towards her, and once more taking her hand, he gazed in her beauteous countenance with intense, but melancholy tenderness, then said,—

"My darling Ethelinde, you love your father?"

"Love you, my father," said the simple, the artless girl, looking into his face with an expression which angels might have felt proud to copy; "oh, tell me,

that I may repent and make atonement, what act have I ever committed that should raise so dreadful a thought upon your mind?—Oh, my beloved parent, you never expressed such a cruel doubt of me before. I am your child, your only child, and it were better at once to die than to live without your confidence. Father, father, what have I done to cause you to question me thus?—Tell me for the love of Heaven, or my heart will break!"

Hysterically sobbing, the lovely maiden threw herself upon her parent's bosom, and but for his support, the power of her emotions must have caused her to sink insensible on the floor. He clasped her tenderly in his arms, and was again unable to speak for a few moments. It was evident that some desperate struggle was going forward in his breast.

"My sweet Ethelinde," he said, at length, in a voice of the most impressive affection, "compose yourself. My words may sound strange, harsh, but they are not meant to be so; and you would make, I know, every allowance for them, could you but be acquainted with the feelings that are at present distracting my mind. Oh, that fatal vow! No, no, my darling child, you have ever been the best, the most affectionate, the most dutiful of daughters to me. Sweet prototype of her who is now in heaven, you are my only earthly blessing!"

"And when I cease to be so, dear father," said the poor girl, looking up, somewhat re-assured, though her tears; "may I cease to live. But do not, oh! do not, I beseech you, unless you would break my heart, importune me to that which is revolting to my feelings."

"Ethelinde," said her father, solemnly, "you have said that you have no heart to bestow upon Everard Welford."

"I may respect him, father, but to love him—to look upon him as my future husband—oh! the very thought makes my blood curdle in my veins with horror."

"Strange infatuation!" exclaimed Mr. Clarence; "what should cause you to entertain such an antipathy to Everard? Has he not been your companion from your earliest days?"

"Oh, yes, yes—but ——"

"But what, Ethelinde? Has he not noble qualities?"

"I would fain believe so, and yet I

have fearful doubts, suspicions, which I cannot conquer, which may be unjust, ungenerous, but which I cannot name."

"Has he not wealth?"

"Yes, yes; but my dear father would not, I am certain, sell the happiness of his daughter at any price."

"Is he not accomplished?" demanded Mr. Clarence, somewhat startled and abashed at his daughter's appeal.

"I admit it, dearest father," replied our heroine, a cold shuddering at the same time passing through her frame; "but still I cannot love him."

Mr. Clarence relinquished his daughter's hand, and once more traversed the apartment for a second or two with disordered steps. At length he turned to her, and in a voice half choked with emotion, said,—

"Ethelinde, would you see your father reduced to ruin, to beggary?"

"Oh, no, no, no!" answered our heroine, distractedly.

"Would you have him proclaimed to the world as a perjured villain?"

"Oh, Heaven forbid!" gasped forth Ethelinde; "but that is impossible, it cannot be!"

"So will it be, unless you consent to become the wife of Everard Welford;" exclaimed Major Clarence, emphatically.

"Then Heaven help me!" cried our heroine, as she sank, overpowered and almost insensible, in her chair.

Her father again approached her, and taking her hand, in an impressive tone, said,—

"Ethelinde, you have not been so candid with me as I expected. But my penetration and my fears have for some time discovered your secret. You love another."

The maiden hid her blushing face with her hands, the tears gushed forth between her taper fingers, her bosom heaved violently, but she could not utter a syllable.

"Norman Rayborne—" said her father, significantly.

Poor Ethelinde looked up with a convulsive start and an imploring look; her lips parted, but still no sound escaped them. The name had acted with magic influence upon her heart, and it was plain that that heart responded to the intimation of her father. Yes, in that affectionate heart Norman Rayborne reigned predominant, and neither time nor circumstance could supplant him.

"You love Norman Rayborne,—my child;" added Mr. Clarence, in a tone of melancholy regret.

"Oh, my father," gasped forth the trembling and blushing Ethelinde; "I am but woman, and who shall decry those affections which have their origin in purity and virtue? Is not Norman noble, generous, good?"

"All—all."

"He loves me father!"

"I believe it, Ethelinde;" sighed her father.

"Is he not worthy of me?"

"Oh yes! oh yes!"

"Then why should I discard from my heart the worthy object of its choice?" demanded the lovely girl with energy.

"Oh, God! oh, God!—that I should be compelled by stern necessity to act thus!" groaned Mr. Clarence, striking his forehead. "Ethelinde, my child, reflect—reflect—I admit all that you have said to be correct—incontrovertible; —I acknowledge the great merits of Norman Rayborne! I confess that I would prefer him for the future partner for my child—but—but—he is poor— his fortunes are broken, without any prospect of their—"

"Father," interrupted Ethelinde, with a look of surprise and gentle reproach; "I never, I cannot believe you sordid. Oh, why allude to Norman's poverty, which has been caused by no misconduct of his own, and which he with the aid of an all Merciful Providence, may in the course of a few years be able to redeem."

"Most heartily do I wish that he may," said her father, earnestly; "but you must banish him from your thoughts, Ethelinde."

"Oh, never! never! It is impossible," replied our heroine, energetically.

"He can never become your husband!" said Mr. Clarence, with emotion.

"Then never, never will I become the wife of any other man!" said Ethelinde, firmly.

"Ethelinde! Ethelinde!" cried her father, grasping her arm, with a convulsive emotion, and looking with an expression in her countenance which amounted to horror;—"beware—beware what you say; the character, the fortune of your unhappy father, depends upon your decision."

"Oh, no, no, no!" ejaculated Ethelinde, "it cannot be!—recal that assertion;—how can your character and your fortune be so involved?"

"Ethelinde, my child," replied her father, in a hoarse voice, and shuddering as if some painful recollection was torturing his mind; "you can little imagine the feelings which now distract me;—there is a secret, a fearful secret, which I have never yet disclosed to you, and which compels me to act as I now do. Everard Welford holds me in his power, at his will I rise or fall to a state of degradation from which nothing can ever recover me. I believe he loves you, and—"

"But the secret, father,—the secret?"

Mr. Clarence hesitated, and clasped his burning forehead.

"Not to night, my child," he said, at last. "I feel inadequate to the task, but to-morrow you shall know all."

"Oh, why keep me in suspense?" said our heroine imploringly.

"Spare me, Ethelinde," said her father, "wait but till the morning, and then I will reveal everything, and throw myself upon your mercy and forbearance."

"Oh, my father," exclaimed Ethelinde, "I beseech you talk not thus. What can be the nature of this dreadful secret that you should thus recoil from the task of disclosing it? My revered parent, I am convinced, could never have done anything that he should be ashamed to acknowledge."

"Hold! hold! Ethelinde," said Mr. Clarence, "you torture me. Were it not for the fatal passion you entertain towards Norman Rayborne, I might be spared this trial; I might be saved from humiliation. A fatal vow many years since passed my lips, extorted under peculiar circumstances, which has ever since embittered my days, and from which I have not the power to absolve myself. To-morrow you shall know all; but meanwhile reflect seriously and solemnly upon what I have said, and endeavour to look upon Everard with a more favourable eye, and to subdue the unfortunate affection you entertain towards his rival, who leaves this neighbourhood to-morrow, and whom you may never behold again. Heaven bless you, my sweet girl;—retire to your chamber, and endeavour to tranquilise your feelings. Good night—good night."

He embraced his daughter affectionately, and with the utmost emotion, and then, without waiting for any reply, abruptly quitted the room.

Ethelinde covered her face with her hands, and then remained for a few minutes in a state of the utmost amazement and confusion at all that she heard.

"Good God!" she exclaimed, at last, "what can be the nature of this dreadful secret; and how can my father have compromised himself in the manner he has hinted at? Love Everard Welford, —forget Norman Rayborne! Oh, never, never—it is impossible! My heart revolts at the bare idea. There is something in the character of Everard which makes me look upon him with a sensation of dread, while in proportion does my affection for his noble hearted rival increase. True, he is poor, he is unfortunate—but, oh! how rich in mental endowments. To-morrow he leaves the country to follow his precarious fortunes, and I may never more behold him. I have promised to meet him under the seventh oak tree in the dell to-night, and shall I break my word, and render him more wretched than the thought of separation at present makes him? No, I cannot, let the consequences be whatever they may. Heaven teach me how to act."

She clasped her hands and raised her tearful eyes as she thus spoke, and remained for some time unable to utter another word. She had never yet disobeyed the will of her father, and deeply did it grieve her to be compelled to do so on the present occasion; but the ardent sentiments she entertained towards Norman Rayborne left her no alternative. She could not abandon the idea of keeping her appointment, notwithstanding all that her father had said to her.

After the lapse of a few minutes more, she retired to her apartment, where she endeavoured to compose her feelings, and to muster fortitude to fulfil the engagement she had made with her lover.

A neighbouring church clock, at length

struck the half hour after nine, and Ethelinde arose from her seat, and hastily throwing on her bonnet and shawl, opened her room door, and listened attentively on the landing to ascertain whether any person was stirring. All was silent, and she stepped lightly and quickly down the stairs; but when she came to the door of her father's apartment, she was compelled to pause, and could not help trembling when she heard him pacing his room, with disordered steps, and muttering incoherent words to himself.

Mentally she invoked a blessing upon his head, and then with fresh courage, she passed on her way, and soon found herself in the open air.

Ten o'clock was the hour at which she had promised to meet her lover, and she had therefore no time to lose. She quickened her speed, and took the nearest way to the place of assignation.

The silvery moon illumined all around, and the air was serene and beautiful, and refreshing after the heat of the day.

Ethelinde felt her spirits somewhat revive as she proceeded, and a ray of hope dawned upon her mind, notwithstanding that was the last time she would see Norman for an uncertain period if in fact, they should ever meet again. The following morning, driven by poverty he was about to leave his native land, and to be exposed to all the perils of the deep, and the agony of Ethelinde at the thought, especially under the circumstances, needs no description. She was left without the chance of endeavouring to inspire him with hope, and what would be his anguish when he was made acquainted with what had taken place between her and her father? She could never find resolution to impart it to him, and at length determined, if possible, to remain silent on the painful subject.

The seventh oak-tree in the dell had ever been the lovers' trysting-place, and many happy moments had they there passed together, moments such as our heroine sadly feared they would never experience again.

As she proceeded, she frequently looked back, apprehensive that she might be watched, and when she reflected on the injunctions of her father, her heart misgave her, and she was half inclined to turn back, but still she had given her promise to Norman, and on so important an occasion—perhaps, the last favour he would ever have an opportunity of asking her, probably the last time that they would have the chance of communicating their thoughts to each other, of repeating those vows they had so often poured into each other's ears, and derived bliss unspeakable therefrom—it would be ungenerous, it would be cruel to disappoint him, and to leave him to proceed on his precarious voyage with his mind overclouded by despair. She committed herself to the guidance of Providence, and determined to proceed.

The moon shone more brightly than ever, and seemed to encourage her, by its chaste and cheering rays, on her way; but still a heavy weight pressed upon the lovely maiden's heart, and seemed to bear her down.

And how could it be otherwise, poor girl, after the interview with her father, the suspense and anxiety she was kept in to know the secret he had to divulge to her,—and the certainty that she was about to separate from, perhaps never to meet again, one whom she loved as dearly as her very existence?

"No, dear Norman," she ejaculated, while the tears trembled in her eyes, and emotions even more powerful than before, throbbed her bosom; "I will not break my word with you on this particularly trying occasion, let the consequences be to me whatever they may. Oh, God!— and yet—" she added with a shudder— "what can be the meaning of my father's words? Can it indeed be true that unless I consent to become the wife of Everard Welford, misery, ruin, and degradation will descend upon his head?— Dreadful thought! It cannot be! It must be a mistake;—my dear father, who has ever been so kind and indulgent to me, must be labouring under some fearful delusion! Would to Heaven that he had imparted to me the secret this night, that I might have been guided in my actions."

Ethelinde paused, and a trembling sensation, a sort of presentiment, came over her mind; but at that moment the old clock chimed forth the three quarters past nine, and reminded her that she had not an instant to lose.

She bounded forward with renewed courage; all other thoughts were absorbed in that of meeting her lover, and hearing from his lips those words of affection she had so often listened to with such infinite delight. But still, as she proceeded, the observations of her father that evening rushed with the most vivid force upon her memory. But to love Everard Welford—to become his bride! Oh, that was impossible! Sooner than make such a bitter sacrifice of her hopes and feelings—sooner than abandon Norman—the dear, the noble-minded Norman, she could die. Life without him would be insupportable!

Ethelinde now descended a hill, from the summit of which a view of the dell might be obtained, and was soon fast approaching the well-remembered place of appointment, the seventh oak tree.

Still more brightly shone the moon, and Ethelinde could see everything for some distance, as clear as if it had been at noon-day. Her heart beat violently against her side, with the power of her emotions and timid anticipations, especially when she caught a glimpse of a figure which she took to be that of her lover, moving between the trees.

Ethelinde hastened forward, and the next moment was clasped fondly in the arms of him who looked upon her with complete adoration.

And Norman Rayborne was, indeed, both as regarded his personal attractions and mental qualifications, well worthy to become the husband of such a maiden as Ethelinde Clarence. His figure was tall and graceful, possessing an air of nobility and dignity that could not fail to attract the attention at first sight. His countenance was open, intelligent, and handsome. His eyes spoke the language of a mind that was endowed with every manly virtue.

Norman's father, who had been a clergyman, was no more, and unfortunately, owing to the failure of a suit at law, he had left his widow, the amiable Mrs. Rayborne, her son and daughter, the simple, artless, and beautiful Kate, in very indifferent circumstances. A friend of his late father having procured a situation in the East Indies for him, which was likely, in the course of time, to turn out a lucrative one, he was to depart, the morning ensuing the night of which we are writing; and many a pang did it cost him, not only the thoughts of being separated from his beloved Ethelinde, but to leave his mother and sister behind unprotected, and almost friendless.

From childhood Norman and Ethelinde had resided in the same neighbourhood, and an intimacy had sprung up between them which soon ripened into affection. But although the greatest friendship had existed between the families of Major Clarence and the Reverend Mr. Rayborne, the former evidently divined the sentiments of Norman and his daughter towards each other with regret, and so far from encouraging, did all he possibly could to stifle them; while, on the other hand, he did all that was in his power to rivet the affections of Ethelinde on Everard Welford.

Everard was the only son of a wealthy father, who, like Mr. Clarence had been for some time left a widower, and between the two gentlemen there existed a friendship of a most peculiar and mysterious description, of which more anon. However, it was quite certain that Mr. Welford possessed a most extraordinary influence over our heroine's father, and that he was fearful of offending him; the cause of which will be explained at some future occasion.

Everard Welford was handsome, accomplished, and prepossessing in his manners, but still, although she could not account for it, Ethelinde for some time had been unable to look upon him without a feeling approaching to dread, and consequently the agony she endured when his company was forced upon her, and she was compelled to listen to sentiments and protestations to which her heart could not respond, may be readily imagined. But to return to the meeting in the dell.

With rapture Norman pressed the beautious form of Ethelinde to his heart and for some moments the emotions which struggled in the bosoms of both, deprived them of the power of utterance.

"Dearest Ethelinde," at last exclaimed the young man," how can I sufficiently thank you for this condescension; but I was certain on so melancholy occasion, your gentle heart would not suffer you to disappoint me. Ah! Ethelinde, you must imagine the anguish which at present occupies my mind. To-morrow I leave my native land, to be separated from you, my revered mother and beloved sister, perhaps never to meet again. Stern necessity tears me away from all I hold dear on earth, and perchance ere many months have elapsed, my cold remains may be mouldering in a foreign grave."

"Oh, Norman," sighed Ethelinde, fixing her beautiful eyes with an expression of ungovernable affection upon his countenance; "talk not thus. Many—many happy years, I trust, are in store for you. You will return to your home under more prosperous circumstances than those you leave it under, and,——"

"And do you wish it, sweet Ethelinde?" eagerly asked her lover.

"Norman," replied Ethelinde, in a tone of surprise and gentle reproach, "can you doubt the sincerity of my good wishes towards you? —The respect I bear towards you, and the deep interest I feel in your welfare?—And yet—" she added hesitatingly, and averting her blushing countenance from the gaze of him she addressed.

"And yet what, Lovely Ethelinde?" he asked, impatiently.

"I would," she faltered out, in a faint and agitated voice, "I would when you are away, Norman, have you endeavour to think of me only with esteem, as—as a sister."

"Forget you, Ethelinde! Oh, little did I ever expect such cruel words from you, especially on so sad an occasion as the present, and it has thrown a sudden blight upon those hopes I have, perhaps, been too presumptuous in entertaining. Tell me, Ethelinde, if you would not drive me to distraction, what have I done to forfeit your love; that love, the confidence of possessing which, has sustained me through all the many vicissitudes I and my family have had to encounter?"

"Oh, nothing, nothing, Norman," vehemently replied Ethelinde; "believe me, no change has taken place in my sentiments; but fate frowns upon us; —my father will not sanction our passion."

"He would have you unite your fate to that of Everard Welford," said Norman; "is it not so, fair Ethelinde?"

"Alas! it is most true," sighed our heroine.

"But can you love him, Ethelinde?"

"Oh, why ask me such a question, Norman?"

"You will never consent to resign your hand to a man you cannot love?"

"Alas! alas!—how can I help myself? My father wills it so, and I dare not disobey him."

Norman struck his forehead with agony, and was for a few moments unable to speak.

"Your father, Ethelinde," he said at length, "can never be so cruel towards a daughter for whom he has ever evinced such powerful affection. I cannot believe it. I think I know Major Clarence's character better. He may reject me at present, in consequence of the wretched state of my fortunes, but Providence may mend them, and surely, since he can raise no objection to my character, he will not persist in withholding his assent to that in which the happiness of his only child is so deeply involved."

"Heaven knows," returned the fair girl, in a voice of melancholy tenderness, "how my wishes coincide with your own, Norman;—but cruel destiny wills that they shall not be gratified; we must endeavour to forget each other in any other character than that of dear friends."

"And you will give your hand to Everard Welford?"

"Alas!—I fear I shall be compelled, if my heart does not break in the struggle with my feelings."

"Oh, misery! misery! But you cannot mean what you say, Ethelinde. You can never consent to such a monstrous sacrifice, neither can your father be so cruel and unjust, or Everard Welford so ungenerous as to exact it. Promise me that you will remain firm in your opposition to such an unnatural demand. I cannot—dare not bid you farewell until you have made me such an assurance."

"Oh, do not urge me, Norman; I must not, dare not comply."

"Then you no longer love, Ethelinde, and I am indeed wretched, hopeless, and accursed!"

"Oh, Norman," sobbed the blushing maiden, "this from you; alas! I love you too well for the happiness of us both. It is most unfortunate that we ever knew each other; then might I not have hesitated to act in obedience with my father's will.   This very evening, my father commanded me to forget you, and to look upon Everard Welford as my future husband.   Nay more, he told me that he was bound by a solemn and fatal vow to bestow my hand on no other than him, and that if I dared to disobey him, it would bring him to misery, ruin, and degradation."

Norman looked at her with the most unaffected astonishment and emotion, as he said,——

THE PARTING OF ETHELINDE AND NORMAN RAYBORNE.

"What mean your words, Ethelinde? There is some extraordinary mystery in this which I cannot fathom."

"There is a secret, Norman, and I fear a dreadful one, which my poor father has promised to disclose to-morrow.   I tremble with suspense to hear it."

Norman again struck his forehead in despair, and paced backwards and forwards with the greatest emotion.

"Oh, God!" he exc'aimed," "never did I expect it would come to this.   But must we part thus Ethelinde?   Must I go to the land of the stranger deprived of every hope?"

"What can I say, Norman?" Ethelinde ejaculated, wringing her hands. "Oh, pity me—pity me!"

"Ethelinde," returned her lover, "I cannot leave this spot, until you have made me a promise."

"Name it, and Heaven knows how willingly I will comply with your request, if it be in my power."

"Promise me then, dear Ethelinde," said Norman, "that in spite of everything, you will not for three years grant your hand to any man, especially Everard Welford. Promise me this, and I will endeavour to be content."

"Oh, Norman, how can you require me to make such a vow? How can I resist the importunities of Everard, and the commands of my father?"

"Then you would drive me to utter despair."

"No, no, no!—this is cruel. How can I struggle against the fate with which I am threatened?"

"Your father will not, cannot be so blind to reason, so insensible to pity, Ethelinde, as to refuse to allow you that short grace. Will you only say that you will beseech him to do so?"

Ethelinde still hesitated, and remained silent for a few minutes, at length she said,—

"May Heaven pardon me if I do wrong; but—but I do promise you, Norman"

"Oh, thanks, thanks!" he cried, "but one more promise, and I have done."

"Do not, I beseech you, urge me further."

"But my happiness or eternal misery depends on this, dear Ethelinde, and I am sure you cannot refuse me. Promise me then, I implore you, that your sentiments towards me shall undergo no change. That at the end of three years should I return safe, and in more prosperous circumstances, you will then, if nothing occurs to prevent it, consent to become my wife."

Once more Ethelinde paused, and Norman fixed upon her an appealing look that seemed as if it would penetrate to her soul. At last her emotions overpowered her, and she threw herself sobbing on his bosom, and for a few moments they were both unable to speak.

"Say but the word, dear Ethelinde," at length exclaimed her lover· "that makes me happy or miserable for ever. Do not keep me in suspense, I beseech you."

"I—I promise, Norman;" said Ethelinde in a faint voice, and the moment she had given utterance to the words, a fearful sensation came over her heart, and she almost repented the promise she had made.

Norman pressed her in transport to his heart, and a terrible weight seemed to be removed from his breast.

"Heaven bless you my beloved Ethelinde for that sweet promise; it will be a constant source of comfort and hope to me when I am far away. On this very day three years then, mark me, I will if I am alive, meet you here at the seventh oak tree, and trust that I may then have the felicity of claiming from you without fear, the fulfilment of your promise."

Most fervently did Ethelinde respond to that wish, but she could not entertain the sanguine hope which animated the bosom of her lover.

They now walked towards the house of Ethelinde's father, conversing upon the subject which was nearest their hearts. The clock had already struck eleven, and our heroine was apprehensive lest her absence should be discovered.

But when the moment came for the lovers to separate, their anguish was more powerful than words can describe it. Again and again they sighed farewell, and embraced, ere they could tear themselves away. But the bitter trial was over, and Ethelinde, entering the house unperceived, hastened to her chamber, where she sank on a chair, completely exhausted and overpowered by the strength of her emotions.

CHAPTER II.

THE DISCLOSURE.—THE FATAL VOW.

SLEEP the fair Ethelinde could not, and it was some time ere she even sought her pillow. Her thoughts were fixed upon her lover, and the parting interview she had had with him, and sometimes she could not help regretting and reproaching herself for the promise she had made to him, and which she could not for the present see that she could possibly fulfil.

And they might never meet again !—Her heart sunk within her at this thought, and earnestly she supplicated Heaven to watch over and protect him from all the dangers to which he might be exposed. That she could ever cease to love him she felt was impossible, and she could not think of a union with Everard Welford without fear and disgust.

And with what trembling anxiety did she await the disclosure which her father had promised to make the following day, and on which, in all probability her fate depended. That it was something terrible, his words seemed undoubtedly to imply, and although she was so anxious she almost feared to hear it.

When sleep at length visited her pillow, the most frightful dreams disturbed her rest, and she awoke at an early hour in the morning unrefreshed.

The sun had arisen and his cheerful beams streamed in at her chamber window. None of the family were yet stirring, and she therefore determined to take a walk for about an hour in the neighbouring fields. Having left the house, she rambled on buried in deep and melancholy thought. She recalled to her memory all that had passed, and she could not restrain her tears when she thought of her separation from Norman Rayborne, and the possibility that they might never meet again, or if they did, that it might be under circumstances she shuddered to contemplate.

She strolled among all those scenes he had most delighted to frequent, and pondered over all he had at different times said, and her mind became more sad the longer she reflected.

She knew that he had before this started on his journey, or, notwithstanding the anguish another parting would cost them, she might have been disposed to have strolled towards his residence.

Tired, however, at length with her walk she slowly retraced her steps towards home.

On her arrival there, she was somewhat surprised to find that her father had partaken of the morning meal, without inquiring after her, and had then left the mansion, leaving no message for her as to the time he should return.

The morning passed away, the afternoon arrived, and still Mr. Clarence came not, and when the evening set in and he was still absent, the astonishment of Ethelinde increased, and she became likewise somewhat alarmed. Independant of this she was most anxious to be made acquainted with the important secret he had promised to impart to her.

At last, however, our heroine's suspense was removed, Mr. Clarence returned, but immediately hastened to his chamber, where he remained secluded for some time, when she received a message from him to attend him in the library.

She trembled so violently as she made her way to the library that she could not without difficulty proceed, and when she reached the door, she was obliged to pause in order that she might somewhat recover herself.

On entering the library, she found her father seated, with his elbow leaning on the table, and his head resting on his hand. He seemed not to have noticed her presence, and she paused, after she had entered a few paces into the apartment and snatched the opportunity, not only to recover her composure, but to contemplate the marked and impressive aspect of her father's countenance.

Frequently, during this brief interval, Mr. Clarence sighed deeply, and Ethelinde could perceive from the painfully nervous feeling that characterised his whole demeanour, the emotions which were passing in his bosom.

Still she hesitated; her light step had not reached his ear, and she feared to disturb him, anxious even as she was to hear the secret he had promised to divulge. She trembled and was almost disposed to retire again from the room, when her father suddenly raised his eyes, started slightly, and the colour left his cheeks for a second or two, as if he had encountered some disagreeable vision.

Ethelinde remained on the spot where she tremblingly stood, until her father had recovered himself sufficiently to speak. He arose from his chair, and in melancholy accents, said,—

"Come hither, my Ethelinde," you have nothing to fear—no more, at least, than what may arise from—be seated, child,—be seated."

Mr. Clarence handed his daughter a chair as he spoke, which our heroine gladly availed herself of. Another pause ensued, the major looking intently at his daughter, as if fearful, and shrinking from the task he had voluntarily imposed upon himself. It was indeed, a severe trial for his feelings.

All the bitter past was struggling and effervescing in his mind;— how terrible were those retrospections; what awful self reproaches did they convey with them. How keenly did he feel the degraded position in which he ought to stand in his lovely daughter's eyes at the exposition he was about to make of his former errors, and by which, loving him as he well knew she did, he must doom her to the blasting of all her youthful hopes, and wishes, and prospects. He felt himself almost inadequate to the fearful revelation, and scarcely dared to raise his eyes towards the countenance of his beaetuous daughter, whose agony of mind was as intense as his own.

Ethelinde could plainly perceive that the nature of that her father had to communicate was of the most dreadful description, and anxious as she was to know the secret that was so oppressively weighing upon his breast, and with which her future destiny and prospects, her hopes, her happiness, her wishes, and probably the only link that held her to life as valuable, were so immediately connected, she would gladly have spared him the pain of the disclosure.

And then again she reflected, with the most agonizing feelings, upon the rash promise she had made to him who held the sole possession of her heart, to whom all her woman's strongest affections were devoted, and she shuddered at the bare idea of the dreadful position in which she might have placed herself; the fatal consequences which might ensue to her and her father.

But surely he could never wish or intend to sacrifice her to one whom she had ever candidly acknowledged she could never, at most, more than esteem as a friend. Everard himself could not be so ungenerous as to persist in demanding the hand of that woman, whose heart was devoted to another. In making the promise she had done at her parting interview with Norman Rayborne, she had only followed the dictates of her own spontaneous and virtuous feelings, and considering the merits of the individual upon whom she had placed her youthful affections, surely she had nothing to reproach herself with? Yet she felt that she had been guilty of a dereliction of duty, and therefore she trembled in the presence of her father.

Mr. Clarence made two or three efforts to speak, but his thoughts overpowered him. He again dropped his head upon his hand, and sighed frequently and deeply. This silence was more torturing to the feelings of Ethelinde than the most painful certainty could have been. It was a dreadful prelude to that which she anticipated. Her heart palpitated at double its natural pace, and her suspense was almost too powerful for endurance.

"Ethelinde, my sweet, my beloved Ethelinde," at length said her father, in accents of the most melancholy tenderness, and affectionately kissing her forehead; "you have told me that you have no heart to bestow upon Everard Welford?"

Ethelinde's bosom throbbed violently, the crimson blushes suffused her cheeks, tears rushed to her eyes,—she tried to speak, but utterance was denied her, and she averted her gaze from that intense one of her father's.

"Alas! alas!" ejaculated Mr. Clarence, "that silence, and what I have before observed, independent of what has fallen from your own lips, my Ethelinde, convince me that I am correct, and show me the full extent of the misery which is in store for me; a severe, but just punishment for my former iniquity."

"Oh, horror! my dear father," exclaimed our heroine, suddenly looking up, and gasping for breath; "say not so; it cannot be,—you must be labouring under some fearful delusion."

"Would to Heaven that I were," returned Mr. Clarence, solemnly, and with an agony of expression that made his daughter's heart sink within her; "how shall I utter, how disclose the fatal truth? How reveal the extent of my shame? Ethelinde, I have been a villain, and it is only by the sacrifice of your feelings, your hopes, your prospects, your probable happiness, that your wretched father can save himself from being denounced to the world in his true character."

Ethelinde stared at him aghast; she could scarcely believe the evidence of her senses, but was almost inclined to think that some strange species of madness had taken possession of his intellects.

"For the love of Heaven, my dear father," she at length cried, "explain yourself. Keep me not, I entreat you, in this horrible state of suspense. My father ever have been guilty of that which he should be ashamed to acknowledge, or have done a single thing which he could not look back upon with pride and self-gratulation?—oh, it is impossible."

"Ethelinde," said Mr. Clarence, shuddering, "this virtuous, this generous confidence tortures me more than all. My sweet child, I am unworthy of your sympathy."

"Gracious Heaven! What can all this mean?" said the astonished and terrified Ethelinde, throwing her arms around her father's neck, and looking in his pale and agitated countenance with an expression that made him shrink appalled. "Father, I implore you, by my mother's sainted spirit, to recal your dreadful words."

"I cannot, I dare not, Ethelinde," groaned the major. "But—but—you love Norman Rayborne?"

"Alas!" sighed the blushing damsel, "would that for your sake, after what you have intimated, my beloved parent, I could love Everard Welford half as fervently."

"Oh, God!" cried Mr. Clarence, striking his forehead, and turning from the affectionate embrace of his daughter with a shudder of horror;—"what a monster I have been!—And must I crush the bright hopes of one so young, so fair, so loving, so dutiful?—Ethelinde, either you must discard Norman Rayborne from your heart, and become the bride of Everard Welford, or your father will be denounced to the world as a villain, the guilty perpetrator of—"

"Of what—of what?" gasped forth our heroine, with choking agony.

"Of a crime which would have consigned him to the gallows, and from which alone a vow—a fatal vow, a vow that dooms you to Everard Welford, rescued him!"

It would be utterly impossible to describe the tone, the appalling tone, in which this astounding, this awful disclosure was made, or the feelings with which Ethelinde received it. For a moment, she looked at her unhappy parent with a wild and vacant stare. Then she grasped his arm with a convulsive motion; her brain swam round; —a mist floated before her eyes, and with a shriek of horror she sank insensible in her parent's arms.

———

CHAPTER. III.

THE FURTHER TRIALS OF THE HEART.

WHEN Ethelinde was restored to consciousness, she found herself in bed, in her own chamber, and her female domestic in attendance upon her. The sun was streaming in at the windows, and, therefore, it was quite evident that she must have been insensible for many hours.

The poor girl passed her fair hand across her forehead, and endeavoured to collect her thoughts. For some minutes only a faint outline of what had transpired at the interview between her and her father, recurred to her memory, like the fragment of some frightful vision, but at length the whole dreadful truth was brought most vividly to her recollection, and starting up in the bed, she stared around her in dismay.

"Oh, God!" she ejaculated, clasping her hands, as the last words of her father flashed upon her fevered brain; "it was not then a dream! Father, unhappy father, where are you? Recal those dreadful words. Where is my father?—assist me to arise, that I may hasten to him, and hear the disavowal from his lips."

"Pray compose yourself, my respected young lady," said Jane, the attendant, "and remaim quietly in bed. Thank Heaven you are at last returned to sensibility. I was afraid that you would never open your eyes upon the world again."

"What is the time?" demanded our heroine, eagerly.

"It is past twelve o'clock, miss," replied Jane, "and you have been in a state of unconsciousness ever since yesterday evening."

"My father!—oh, where is he?"

"He is below, miss, and I must hasten to inform him of your recovery. Pray endeavour to calm your feelings, and I will quickly return."

Ethelinde endeavoured to make some reply, but she was unable, and Jane quitted the chamber.

Ethelinde tried to arise from her couch, but her strength was so enfeebled that she could not, and she sank back on her pillow completely exhausted.

Jane was gone a considerable time, and our heroine was left entirely to her own thoughts; and how agonising, how insupportable were they! The whole of what had transpired at the meeting with her father rushed with overwhelming force upon her memory, and drove her almost to madness and utter despair.

Those awful words were impressed upon her brain in characters of fire:

"Guilty of a crime which would have consigned him to the gallows, and from which alone a vow—a fatal vow, a vow which dooms you to Everard Welford, rescued him!"

Could it be true? Had she not suffered some frightful delusion to take possession of her senses? Oh, no, the fatal truth was too apparent for her to suffer herself to be mistaken! Her father, her amiable, her kind, indulgent father, who was revered by all who knew him, acknowledging himself to have been guilty of a crime by which he had forfeited his life to the offended laws of his country;—the bare thought appeared too monstrous to be credited. Would that she had died ere the dreadful avowal could have passed his lips!

But what was the awful secret?—How anxious was she, yet how she dreaded to hear it! Her heart sank within her, and she awaited the return of her attendant in the most trembling and horrible state of suspense.

And must she then resign all hopes of her beloved, her noble-hearted Norman, after the solemn promise she had made him? Was there no other way of rescuing her unfortunate father from shame and misery, but by sacrificing her hand to Everard Welford? The bare thought brought distraction along with it. And what could be the nature of the vow that could thus so cruelly enfetter her father? Her brain became lost in a chaos of uncertainty!

But no, surely Everard would never persist in enforcing the fulfilment of that vow, when he was assured that he could not possess her heart. She had never given any encouragement to his addresses, and therefore he could not have deceived himself. She would throw herself upon his mercy; she would appeal to his feelings as a man, and surely he could not turn a deaf ear to her. She would even do more, if at the expiration of the three years, Norman Rayborne did not return, or she should not hear from him, she would consider that he had ceased to love her, that she was absolved from her promise, and that she would then, even at the sacrifice of her own happiness, become the wife of Everard Welford!

Surely he could not refuse such a request!—Alas! she knew not sufficient of the character of Everard Welford, the power he held over her father, and the motives which urged him on, or she would never have entertained such an idea even for a moment.

At length, after the lapse of more than a quarter of an hour, which appeared like an age to the impatient and anxious Ethelinde, Jane returned to the chamber.

"My dear father," eagerly ejaculated our heroine, "have you seen him?"

"Oh, yes, miss," answered Jane.

"And what did he say? Where is he? Assist me to dress, that I may hasten to him."

"My dear young lady," remarked the attendant, "I beseech you to compose yourself; your father is not in the house."

"Not in the house?" repeated Ethelinde, with astonishment and emotion.

"No, miss," replied Jane, "he left the mansion immediately after writing this note, which he requested me to deliver to you."

As she uttered these words, Jane produced a note, which Ethelinde eagerly seized, and with a trembling hand unfolding it, read the following words:—

"My Beloved Ethelinde,—Business calls me from home, without the opportunity of seeing you. I may be absent for a day or two, so do not be alarmed.

Oh, my child, for my sake, for your own, endeavour to acquire fortitude to hear the awful secret I have to impart to you, and that Heaven may watch over, protect, and bless you, is the fervent prayer of YOUR UNHAPPY FATHER."

Ethelinde sank back on her pillow, overpowered by surprise, disappointment, and agony. What business could be sufficiently important to call her father away from home at such a critical moment?—And must she then still be kept in her present dreadful state of suspense for an indefinite period?—It was a trial almost too great for her to endure; but tears came to her relief, and after the lapse of another hour or two she was sufficiently recovered to leave her bed and to go below.

Here alone, she gave free indulgence to her feelings, and wept bitterly. Again and again she reflected upon the observations of her father, and endeavoured, but in vain, to disbelieve in their reality. The blood curdled in her veins as she did so, and her brain seemed as if it were on fire.

In the course of that melancholy day, she received a visitor, who was always most welcome to her. It was the lovely and gentle Kate Rayborne, the only sister of him who held possession of her heart, and who loved her as affectionately as if they had been connected by the dearest ties of nature.

A fair girl indeed was Kate Rayborne, and as lovely in mind as she was charming in person. A fit companion for the gentle, but now suffering Ethelinde. They had ever looked upon each other with the affection of sisters, and looked forward with fond and sanguine hopes to that happy day when a union between Norman and our heroine would give them that claim upon each other. Alas! they had little anticipated the cruel disappointment and sufferings which were in store for them.

Kate, as may be imagined, was in great trouble at the departure of her brother from his native land, and naturally concluded that the anguish of Ethelinde sprang from the same melancholy source. How anxious was our afflicted heroine to make her fair friend acquainted with the whole dreadful truth; but she dared not to do so; she found courage sufficient to inform her that her father had posi-

tively commanded her to forget Norman in any other character than that of a friend, and to look upon Everard Welford as her future husband.

However, the keen and penetrating eye of the gentle Kate Rayborne was not to be deceived; she perceived that even some weightier grief was pressing upon her fair friend's heart, and while she deeply sympathised with her in the sorrows which had fallen upon her spring of life, she delicately and feelingly forebore to elicit from her the torturing secret. She felt satisfied that it must be something of the most important and fearful character, or she would not hesitate for a moment to make her her confidant, as she had ever done in all matters nearest her heart.

The two friends remained silent for a few minutes, while tears of genuine feeling and anxiety trembled in their eyes.

"Your excellent father, my dear Ethelinde," at last remarked Kate, "is, I know, generous, kind, and indulgent. He has ever been most studious of your happiness, but—but you cannot, unless I am much mistaken, you do not love Everard Welford?"

"Oh, Kate! Kate!" sighed the agonized girl, "why put such a question?—You know my heart;—it has been fully revealed to you; you know that heart throbs for one alone with a most devoted affection, one who has won it by his virtues, and who must ever hold possession of it, until it shall cease to beat. I have not attempted to disguise my real sentiments from my father, and I am satisfied he would not withhold his sanction, were it not that he was bound in—but pardon me, dear Kate;" she faltered out,—"I dare not, I cannot, proceed further."

Kate threw her fair arms around her lovely companion's neck, and their tears mingled together.

"My poor brother," sobbed Kate at length; "oh, shall I never behold him again? Cruel is the destiny which has divided us, Oh, Ethelinde, had you seen him this morning when he parted from me and his poor mother; had you witnessed the sad, the almost distracting emotions which wrung his heart, the agonizing forebodings which had taken possession of his mind, what would have been your feelings!"

"My own loved Kate," sobbed our beautiful heroine, "spare my feelings, I beseech you. Heaven knows what I have suffered since we separated last night. Kate, Kate, I dare not, I must not tell you all that has transpired subsequent to that separation; but it is in consequence of that, you see me thus distracted, — bewildered. My sweet friend, tell me, how did your amiable mother support this dreadful trial, which deprived her of one of the best of sons?"

"Need I attempt to describe to you, Ethelinde?" replied her companion;— "oh, it was a melancholy parting, the more so, as my poor brother, at the last moment seemed to entertain the most irrepressible misgivings of the future which were in store for us all. He communicated, in confidence to me and my mother all that had transpired between you and him at your last interview, and to me he committed a slight memorial which he requested that you would accept for his sake, and at the same time bade me desire you to remember the solemn compact into which you had entered, and to exert all your energies to struggle with those difficulties by which he feared you would be surrounded, and he trusted that Providence would protect you, and enable you to surmount them."

Ethelinde eagerly took the token from Kate's fair hand; it was merely a simple silver locket, inscribed with the initials of Norman Rayborne's name, but she received it with feelings of greater transport than she would at that moment have received all the treasures of the world. She pressed it fervently to her lips, and tears and sobs completely choked her utterance.

And yet what melancholy feelings of despair weighed upon her mind, as the fearful assertions of her father occurred to her, and she knew the insurmountable barrier that was placed between her and Norman! How did she long, yet could not muster sufficient courage to make Kate acquainted with it. And then the suspense, the dreadful suspense she was in to know the true nature of her father's secret!

Her strength of mind almost sunk beneath the terrible weight of these accumulated thoughts. Could she but have dared to make a confidant of her esteemed friend Kate, what a relief would it have been to her.

Our heroine and Kate Rayborne remained together the whole of the day, and when they separated, Ethelinde's feelings were a little more tranquillised. But, alas, that composure soon evaporated.

She retired at an early hour to her chamber, and taking the locket which had been sent to her, by her lover, from her bosom, pressed it again and again to her lips, and shed torrents of tears over it as she gazed upon it.

"Dear Norman," she ejaculated, "how cruel is the destiny which pursues us. What have we done, that we should either of us be thus punished?— and we may never behold each other again, and, perhaps, it were better that we should not, but still the bare thought is madness. And must I, indeed, become the wife of Everard Welford, whom I can scarcely look upon with feelings of respect? Never! never!—forbid it Heaven, I beseech thee! Rather let me die than suffer me to be brought to so revolting a fate."

She pressed her hands upon her burning temples, and madness seemed about to descend upon her brain.

But could it be true that her father had ever been guilty of that which placed him in so awful and disgraceful a position as he had asserted?—it was impossible!—and yet he would surely never thus have accused himself, unless it had some foundation in truth. The words, the dreadful words he had made use of, again rushed upon her memory— they never could be erased from it, and a cold shuddering ran through her veins, which almost overpowered her.

Another wretched night did poor Ethelinde experience. The present absence of her father added to her poignant agony of mind, and she looked in vain for consolation.

She had promised Kate to visit her and her mother on the following day, if her strength would permit her, and she arose with that intention, as soon as she had finished her morning repast, hoping to derive some consolation from their society.

Ethelinde had scarcely dressed herself, however, with that intention, when to her utter confusion and dismay, Everard Welford was announced.

She trembled in every limb;—turned ghastly pale, and for a few moments, so great was her agitation she was unable to speak. When she did, however, in some measure recover herself, she would fain have excused herself from the dreaded interview on the plea of indisposition; but fearful of the consequences which might ensue to her unfortunate father, she reluctantly and fearfully yielded.

"Heaven sustain me," she gasped

ETHELINDE OVERWHELMED BY THE THREATS OF EVERARD WELFORD.

forth, when Jane had retired from the room, "and give me fortitude to support this additional trial. Oh, Everard, if you really entertain the sentiments towards me which you profess to do, you will not persist in your suit. I will appeal to your feelings, and if fortune does not entirely desert me, I shall succeed. Oh, God! What can be the purport of Everard's present visit during the absence of my father?"

She sunk in her chair, and covering her face with her hands, sobbed deeply. In this position Everard Welford found her on his entrance, and he stood for a moment or two, and contemplated her in silence.

Everard Welford was not yet destitute of feeling, but he possessed many evil passions which combatted strongly and successfully with the better portion of his nature.

He had ever felt what he considered to be an ardent and sincere affection towards Ethelinde; but it was indeed a sentiment that was not at all allied to genuine love. Knowing the power that he and his father held over Major Clarence, he had accustomed himself to look with too much confidence on the possession of Ethelinde as a matter of necessity, if not of absolute right.

The coldenss our heroine had evinced towards him, especially latterly, had severely mortified his pride; and the love which evidently existed between her and Norman Rayborne, had excieed his utmost jealousy; but now that obstacle was removed by the departure of his rival from the country, he flattered himself with the idea of the certain and speedy consummation of his wishes.

It was with these impressions upon his mind, that he had seized the opportunity of the absence of Mr. Clarence from the mansion to seek an interview with Ethelinde.

Hitherto he had not troubled himself to confess his passion towards her, thinking that she could not be ignorant of his pretensions, and knowing that it was an understood thing, settled indissolubly between himself, his father, and Major Clarence; but on this occasion he determined to be more explicit, and to make Ethelinde acquainted with the real position in which she stood.

And yet, notwithstanding all his confidence, Everard Welford somewhat shrank from the task he had imposed upon himself, especially when he beheld the state of misery and agitation which Ethelinde was at present evidently enduring. As for our heroine, herself, she ventured not to raise her eyes on the entrance of him she dreaded so much to meet, and her heart palpitated with an emotion which was almost insupportable.

Everard at length approached her, and in a tone of tenderness repeated his name. She started at the sound of his voice, as if awakened from some frightful dream, to the more terrible reality, and on seeing Everard's eyes intently fixed upon her, she shuddered. The expression did not escape his observation, but he was fully prepared for it, and he stifled his real feelings as well as he could, while he said:—

"You turn from me, Ethelinde, the companion of your earliest childhood, with a feeling of repugnance. Is there, then, anything so hateful in my character or appearance, that you should thus shudder in my presence?"

Ethelinde gathered a little fortitude, as she thus faintly replied:—

"The company of Everard Welford has ever hitherto been welcome to me as a friend."

"As a friend!" he repeated, with difficulty restraining his feelings, and concealing his chagrin. "That is rather a cold term, methinks, fair Ethelinde, to apply to one who has stood in the position to you that I have."

"Oh, spare me, Mr. Welford, I beseech you," said Ethelinde, with a look of the most earnest and impressive supplication. "Why torture me with this interview at such a time? I am at present overwhelmed with grief."

"At the departure of young Norman Rayborne from his native land," added Everard, in bitter accents; "I perfectly understand you, Ethelinde; were it Norman Rayborne who now stood before you, instead of Everard Welford, you would be all smiles and gladness."

Ethelinde fixed upon him a look which ought to have melted his very soul, as he uttered these words. She tried to speak, but the words of reproach she would fain have given utterance to, were stifled in her throat. She burst into tears, and again covered her face with her hands.

Everard remained silent for a short time, but it was evident that the emotion of our heroine had a contrary effect upon him to that which it should have done, and rather served to increase his vexation and disappointment.

At last he once more approached her and attempting to take her hand, he said, in more subdued tones,—

"Ethelinde, I do not believe that you could have thought me so blind, as not for some time to have read your sentiments towards Norman Rayborne. Yes,

I nave watched the progress of your passion narrowly, and the indifference and contempt with which you every day beheld me. With much greater forbearance than could have been expected from me under the circumstances, I have watched that fatal passion which can never be gratified. But the time has arrived when a proper understanding must be effected between us. Norman Rayborne has quitted his native land, to which he may never return; he probably will soon learn to forget you, and to place his affections upon some other damsel, more suited to his circumstances in life than Ethelinde Clarence; but whether or no, you must cease to remember him, for it is impossible that you can ever become his wife."

"And by what right does Mr. Welford presume to talk to me thus, in the absence of my father?" demanded our heroine firmly, and her bosom swelling with feelings of indignation and wounded pride, at the presumptuous boldness and confidence of Everard's address.

"Ethelinde," he replied, not at all abashed by her looks, "this is probably not the time to question the right upon which I rest my claims; but rest assured that I make no empty boast when I say that it is powerful, it is insurmountable. Conquer your feelings and prejudices, Ethelinde, and listen to me with patience and indulgence. I come to offer you the homage of a heart which has long been entirely devoted to you, and to avow a passion which even your scorn and neglect has only served to strengthen; a passion which nothing can subdue. I would——"

"Oh, cease, cease," ejaculated the agitated Ethelinde, interrupting him;— "I cannot listen to the confession of sentiments which I feel it is impossible for me ever to return. If you have any respect for my feelings, Everard Welford; —if you would still retain my friendship, you will no longer urge a suit to which my heart will not permit me to give any encouragement."

"And think you, haughty damsel," said Everard, unable any longer to conceal his rage, "that I will so readily resign my pretensions to one whom I have ever been taught to believe as bound to become mine?"

"Bound to become yours?" gasped forth our heroine; and when she recalled to her mind the fearful assertions of her father, she shuddered with horror, and was unable to proceed.

"Aye, bound to me, Ethelinde," replied Everard, "and that by a compact the nature of which you can form no conception of. You are my affianced bride from infancy, and nothing but death can prevent our union."

"What compact can bind me to an union with a man I cannot love?" demanded Ethelinde, once more summoning a little fortitude to her aid.

"Be not obstinate, Ethelinde, or bitterly will you have cause to repent your folly. I would spare your feelings, but your scorn will urge me to say that which I would fain should never pass my lips."

"If you would really spare my feelings, already sufficiently wounded, you will leave me, and think better of what you have already said. Oh, do so! I earnestly implore you. It is not by dark hints and threats that you can hope to advance your suit."

"No, Ethelinde, I have too long delayed—I have too long endured your neglect without murmuring, and witnessed the favour with which you received the addresses of Norman Rayborne, who must henceforth be a stranger to you."

"Sooner would I perish!" exclaimed our heroine, resolutely, "than a promise so revolting to my feelings should pass my lips.

"Ethelinde beware!" said Everard, fixing his eyes full upon her countenance, "you know not the danger you incur by this obstinacy. Bethink yourself ere it is too late."

"Alas! and is this the man who would win my love?" sighed Ethelinde. "Everard Welford, I have listened to you too long, and if you had a spark of manly feeling, you would immediately retire, and not again urge a passion which my heart cannot recognise."

"You view me with hatred, Ethelinde?"

"I would fain view you with friendship, as the friend and companion of my childhood."

"And yet you must become my bride," said Everard.

"Never," returned our heroine, but

when the observations of her father flashed upon her brain, her voice faltered, and she again burst into tears. But Everard had anticipated all this expression of emotion, and he remained unmoved.

"Ethelinde," he said, at length, "I once more caution you to conquer your repugnance, and to listen to my vows with a favourable ear. The love I feel for you is ardent and sincere, and neither time nor circumstance can alter it; have you ever found me unworthy of you? why then should you thus treat me with scorn and neglect?"

"I do not scorn you, Everard; I repeat," replied Ethelinde, looking up through her tears, "I have ever treated you with becoming respect, but I cannot regard you in the character of my future husband. Surely then, you would not possess the hand of one whose heart cannot accompany it."

Everard bit his lips, and took two or three hasty strides across the room, whilst Ethelinde remained in a state of the most trembling anxiety and suspense.

At length he turned towards her and said :—

"Ethelinde Clarence, will no persuasion have any effect upon you?"

"I will never make a promise my heart repudiates;" answered Ethelinde.

"Then mark me;" said Everard, advancing nearer towards her, and grasping her arm, "mark me, obstinate girl! if you persist in rejecting my suit, your father's honour, fortune, nay, probably his life, will pay the penalty of your obstinacy!"

This dreadful confirmation of her father's assertions had the most terrible effect upon the mind of the hapless Ethelinde. Several times she essayed to speak, but in vain. She stared at Everard Welford aghast, but with an expression of the keenest reproach, not unmingled with that of supplication. Strange and terrific thoughts crowded upon her imagination; giddiness seized her brain, and with one despairing cry of the most indescribable agony she sank senseless upon the floor.

———

CHAPTER IV.

THE LOCKET.—THE ACCIDENT, AND PAINFUL CONSEQUENCES TO MAJOR CLARENCE.

WHEN Ethelinde recovered to sensibility, she found herself reclining upon a sofa, and attended upon by the faithful Jane and another servant. She looked anxiously around the room; all that had passed darted at once upon her memory, but Everard was not present, and that afforded her great relief. She inquired whether Mr. Welford had quitted the house, and Jane replied in the affirmative.

"Thank Heaven!" ejaculated our heroine, for the moment not thinking of the presence of the servants, "oh, that I might never behold him again. Oh, my poor father—" but suddenly recollecting herself, she added,—"leave me—I am better now, and wish to be alone."

Jane and her fellow servant immediately obeyed, and retired from the room, and when they were gone, Ethelinde gave full vent to the feelings, the torturing feelings which overpowered her, in a copious flood of tears, which somewhat relieved her overcharged heart.

She ruminated with the most poignant anguish and horrible forboding upon every word which Everard Welford had uttered, and especially after the dark hints her father had thrown out, she could not help perceiving that greater, far greater trials than any she had hitherto experienced were in store for her. Must she then forfeit her vows to Norman Rayborne, who held possession of her heart's dearest affections, and become the wife of a man whom she could now scarcely look upon with any other feeling than one of loathing and disgust? The thought was horrible,—it was most revolting; death presented far less horrors to her imagination than such a cruel sacrifice of her heart's dearest wishes and hopes. And yet she must either yield to this, or according to what her father had stated, and Everard had confirmed, she must consign the former to shame, ruin, nay, even death!

Good God! how dreadful was that thought;

And what could be the nature of the secret which thus placed her father at the mercy of Mr. Welford and his son? Her bewildered brain whirled round, as she in vain endeavoured to form a conception of it.

Her father had been guilty of a crime, according to his own acknowledgment, by which his life was forfeited to the laws of his country. Could it be possible that Everard and his father held that precious life in their hands? Oh, God! by what fatal means had he thus become involved? How could he, so good and amiable, ever have committed himself in so awful a manner?

The dreadful mystery was totally impenetrable! She trembled, yet felt a fearful longing to have the secret divulged to her. She clasped her hands in the agony of her feelings, and sinking on her knees, exclaimed, while she fervently raised her tearful eyes towards Heaven:—

"Father of Mercy, I humbly but earnestly implore thee to advert the evils which I too plainly perceive are impending over me; and if my beloved father has indeed been guilty, to pardon him, and rescue him from the fate to which his enemies would consign him. Oh, spare him and me from the cruel destiny with which we are threatened."

She arose from her knees, and for some time remained totally absorbed in the bitter anguish of her own thoughts. She felt herself totally incapable of fulfilling the engagement she had entered into with Kate Rayborne, although she stood so much in need of the consolation and advice of her and her mother. She was entirely left alone, and on so momentous an occasion she could not imagine what could be the cause of her father's absence from home, and he had given her no means of imagining when he would return, notwithstanding he must be fully aware of the intense anxiety and suspense she must be enduring to know the dreadful secret he had promised to impart to her, and on which her future happiness depended.

After her interview with Everard Welford, she in vain endeavoured to encourage the slightest hope, but looked forward to the worst; still it would have been better at once to be made acquainted with everything than to be kept in that dreadful state of surmise, doubt, and uncertainty.

That she had nothing whatever to hope from the forbearance of Everard she was now thoroughly convinced, and altogether she saw herself involved in a maze of difficulty and danger from which it would be impossible to extricate herself. Again she earnestly implored the Almighty to interpose between her and the fate with which she was threatened! for to be forced to become the wife of Everard Welford, would be to consign her to a doom the horror of which nothing whatever could equal. She now saw his real character as plainly as if it had been reflected in a mirror before her eyes, and though she could, and did at one time esteem him for the many manly qualities he displayed, she now saw that he had only been acting the part of the hypocrite, and he became to her an object of terror and disgust.

To look upon such a man then in the character of her future husband, was a thought to revolting to dwell upon; and yet in spite of all her efforts to banish it, it would continue to flash upon her brain with terrible force; the more so as the mysterious power which Everard and his father evidently possessed over her unfortunate parent, became more apparent to her.

And now the poor girl thought upon the promise, the solemn promise she had made to Rayborne, on the night of their parting, and the dreadful consequences which would probably ensue should she be compelled to break that vow; and her heart was full to bursting.

Oh, what would be his feelings did he but know her present sufferings, and the fearful fate that was impending o'er her head?—anguish the most intense he knew she must be enduring at their separation, so well was he assured of the fervour, sincerity, and purity of her love; but, of course, he could form no conception of her real situation, nor had she any means of making him acquainted with it. One thing, however, she at last resolved upon, painful though it would be to her feelings, namely, to confide all that she at present knew to Kate Rayborne and her mother, for it was from them alone that she could look for solace and advice; it was to those dear friends she could alone venture to disburden her thoughts, it was from them only she could expect sympathy under the numerous and unprecedented troubles which now afflicted her.

And yet how grieved would they be to discover the probability, the more than probability, of the destruction of those fond hopes which she and Norman had cherished in their bosoms, and on the realisation of which their sole happiness, all that made them think life desirable, depended.

To the amiable Mrs. Rayborne our heroine was as much attached as if she had been her own mother, and indeed that excellent woman had ever evinced the same affection towards her as if she had been her child. Sanguine hope had long led her to look upon Ethelinde in the character of her future daughter, and therefore her present disappointment would naturally be more severe than it otherwise would have been.

Ethelinde took from her bosom the locket which had been sent to her by Norman, and while she pressed it again and again to her lips, tears of the most heartfelt anguish streamed from her eyes, and the most agonizing sobs escaped her bosom. He was now far away, exposed to all the dangers of the ocean, and even if he arrived safe at the place of his destination, a far distant land would divide them, perhaps for ever; or what was more horrible still, he might return to find that she had broken her promise, that she had been compelled by remorseless fate, and not her own will to do so, and to find her the broken-hearted victim of that man whom she could now only loathe and despise.

What madness did these reflections inflict upon our beauteous but unfortunate heroine. Her strength almost sunk beneath the oppressive, the insupportable weight. How fervently did she pray to Heaven to interpose in her behalf, or to take her to itself.

She looked in vain for consolation; there was none to be found. All before her was as dark and as gloomy as the dreariest night. The threats of Everard Welford filled her with the utmost alarm, and she had not the least doubt that he would persist in carrying them into effect; and what power had she to offer any resistance? How could she for a moment attempt to do so, if her father's honour, nay, his life were at stake?— She could not repress a groan as these thoughts rushed upon her and threatened to overwhelm her; and for some time she gave herself up entirely to all the harrowing feeling of despair.

She much dreaded another visit from Everard, and she felt certain that it would not be long ere he again thrust himself into her presence, and insulted her ears with his odious importunities. Her last interview with him proved to her that he was quite destitute of that delicate feeling, and manly forbearance for which she had once given him credit; and he had certainly not at all endeavoured to conceal his real intentions. Oh, how sincerely did she wish that her and her father were far removed from the neighbourhood, and where he might not be able to discover them.

Another dreary day passed away, and still Mr. Clarence did not return, nor did Ethelinde hear anything from him. She became more uneasy than before, and unable to account for his protracted absence, was fearful that some accident had befallen him. Surely he might have left word whither he was going, and then she might have been able to communicate with him. His conduct was altogether inexplicable, especially when he must be aware of the dreadful state of anxiety she would be in.

Towards the evening she was again visited by Kate Rayborne, who was fearful that she was ill, as she had not fulfilled her engagement, by visiting her and her mother.

Kate found her young and lovely friend in tears, and immediately exerted herself to the utmost to console her; but it was some time ere she could bring her to anything like a degree of composure.

When, however, Ethelinde found strength sufficient to relate to Kate what had transpired at her late interview with Everard Welford, with what attention did that affectionate girl listen to her, and with what feelings of unfeigned surprise and terror when she mentioned the dark hints thrown out by Everard respecting her father. For some moments she remained wrapt in mute silence and astonishment, then she threw herself into the arms of Ethelinde, and mingled her tears with her's. She saw at once that all the fond hopes which Ethelinde and her brother had entertained towards each other were annihilated, and she foreboded the utmost misery to them both.

"Oh, dear Ethelinde," she ejaculated at last, "this cannot be true;—it must be some cruel invention of Everard's to forward his designs. The story is most improbable, it is impossible. Of what could you excellent father ever have been guilty that he should be placed in so dangerous a predicament?—Banish it from your thoughts my sweet friend, for depend upon it it is all a scandalous and infamous falsehood."

Ethelinde shook her head mournfully. "Would to Heaven that I could think so, dear Kate," she said;—"What an insupportable weight would it remove from my mind. But alas!—my unfortunate father has acknowledged to me the same, and I am left alone to misery and despair."

"Good God!" cried Kate, "can I believe the evidence of my ears?—Your father surely could not have meant what he said. He must have been suffering under some painful excitement at the time, which deprived him of his reason."

"Ah! no, Kate, he spoke it solemnly and deliberately. Oh, my kind friend, pity me, for I am indeed now a most wretched being, and it would be a blessing if Heaven would release me from my sufferings and take me to itself."

"Need I say how much I feel for you dear Ethelinde?" said Kate, "my anguish can scarcely be exceeded by your own. I am lost in amazement."

"Listen to me, Kate," said our heroine, "and you will then be able to judge what ample cause I have to despair." She then related, as well as her sobs and tears would permit her, what had taken place at the meeting between her and her father; and when she came to that part where her father had accused himself of having been guilty of a crime by which, if it was revealed, his life would be sacrificed to the laws of his country, and the power which Mr. Welford and his son held over him, the emotion of Kate became almost as powerful as her own.

Still she could scarcely bring herself to believe in the truth of this singular and dreadful disclosure. She had ever entertained the highest opinion of the character of Major Clarence, and she could not suppose him ever to have been guilty of a single action which he should be ashamed to acknowledge to the world. Altogether, it was a mystery of the most painful description, and she became lost in amazement and uncertainty as she reflected upon it. She conquered her emotions as well as she could, however, and endeavoured to comfort and re-assure Ethelinde, in which she at last, to some little extent succeeded.

The two friends remained together until the deepening shadows warned Kate that it was time to depart. She then arose, and having embraced our heroine affectionately, took her leave, Ethelinde having again promised her, if her health and spirits permitted her, to visit her and her mother on the following day. Indeed Ethelinde was most anxious to see Mrs. Rayborne, that she might pour all her sorrows into her sympathising bosom, and benefit by her friendly advice.

Another night of misery did Ethelinde pass, but by the morning she had so far conquered her emotions, as to appear comparatively tranquil.

She partook hastily of the morning repast, and then proceeded to depart to the house of Mrs. Rayborne, lest she should be again so disagreeably interrupted as she had been the day before.

She left word with Jane whither she was gone, in case her father should return, and then, unattended, commenced her walk, the residence of Mrs. Rayborne being little more than a mile from the mansion.

On her arrival there, Mrs. Rayborne greeted her with motherly affection, and the melancholy expression of her countenance showed how deeply she sympathised with the poor girl in her misfortunes.

Kate had revealed to her mother all that Ethelinde had disclosed to her,—and that good lady, as may be imagined, was not a little shocked and astonished. The circumstances were so mysterious and so painful that they were almost past belief, and Mrs. Rayborne would willingly, if she could have done so, have persuaded herself that it was all a delusion. She felt for Mr. Clarence, whom she much respected, and bitterly did she feel for poor Ethelinde, who by it would be plunged into such misery. Nor was her sorrow and regret less excited in regard to her son, whose hopes would now be entirely annihilated.

Notwithstanding that Mr. Clarence had hitherto withheld his sanction to the passion of Norman and Ethelinde, Mrs. Rayborne had ventured to encourage a hope that the day would come when he would relent, and there would then be no further obstacle to the union of two individuals, who in every respect, both personally and mentally, were so well worthy of each other.

Mrs. Rayborne was so overwhelmed by these melancholy thoughts, that it was some time before she knew how to advise her youthful and lovely visitor. It fact, it was a most arduous task, where the circumstances were so painfully intricate and delicate.

She tried, however, all that she could, by argument to console Ethelinde, and to inspire her with the hope that, notwithstanding the alarming state in which matters at present stood, a wise and all merciful Providence would not suffer such dreadful consequences to take place as she anticipated.

Ethelinde endeavoured to think so, and gradually her feelings became more calm, and she listened to the gentle advice of Mrs. Rayborne with the most fervent attention.

They were suddenly interrupted, however, by the entrance of a servant, who announced that a man had arrived in great haste from the mansion, and wished to see Miss Ethelinde immediately. Our heroine started from her seat in great agitation, and her heart palpitated violently.

"It must be my dear father who has returned," she said, "let me see the messenger instantly."

"Compose yourself, my dear girl," said Mrs. Rayborne, in her kindest accents; but she had scarcely made use of the observations, when George, the servant of Mr. Clarence, was ushered into the room.

His countenance was pale, and he altogether appeared to be in a state of great trepidation. Ethelinde gazed at him intently, and at that moment she felt as if her worst forebodings were all but realized.

"Now, George, tell me quickly, what is the message you have to deliver to me?" she said eagerly. "Your master——"

George looked more disconcerted than before, and hung his head, without returning any answer.

Ethelinde's agony was intense, for she saw at once that the servant had some unpleasant intelligence to deliver.

"Be explicit, George," interposed Mrs. Rayborne, "you see the state of agitation your young mistress is in, and, therefore, at once deliver the message that is entrusted to you. Has Major Clarence returned home?"

"Alas! alas!" replied George, ominously shaking his head.

"Ah!" ejaculated Ethelinde, "my fears are realised;—some accident has befallen my dear father; tell me, George, as you value my future favour, keep me no longer in suspense, what has taken place?"

"Alas! alas! Miss;" replied the man, shaking his head, and looking, if possible, more dismal than before; "you have indeed too truly guessed it; my poor master——"

"What of him?" gasped forth Ethelinde, scarcely able to support herself; "What is the matter?"

"My poor master," returned the servant, "has had the misfortune to be thrown from his horse on his return home, and his head is wounded badly."

"Oh, God! oh, God!" groaned our heroine, in the greatest agony, and she almost sank insensible with the power of her emotions. Mrs. Rayborne and her lovely daughter immediately came to her aid, and by their soothing influence, somewhat tranquilised her feelings.

"My dear girl," said Mrs. Rayborne, "pray be firm; after all, your poor father's accident may not be of the dangerous nature which you seem to anticipate. But we are delaying time. Come, Ethelinde, I will accompany you home, and Heaven grant that we may find your revered parent in no danger."

Tears came to the relief of Ethelinde, she instantly aroused herself, and having thrown on her bonnet and shawl, took the arm of her kind friend Mrs. Rayborne, and immediately quitted the house, the servant having preceded them.

On the way to the mansion of Major Clarence, Mrs. Rayborne and her young friend exchanged but few words, but the agony of Ethelinde, in spite of all her efforts to restrain it, was most intense. She formed the most terrible ideas of the nature of the injury her beloved father had received, which Mrs. Rayborne in vain endeavoured to combat, and she trembled so violently, that had it not been for the support of Mrs. Rayborne's arm, she must frequently have sunk to the earth.

They were not long in arriving at the mansion, and found the servants in a state of the greatest confusion and ex-

citement. Jane met them immediately on their entrance, and her looks added to the apprehensions of our heroine.

"Oh, Jane, tell me," she ejaculated in a hurried tone," how is my poor father? —But let me at once hasten to his chamber and ascertain the truth. I fear, alas! from all that I perceive, that the accident is of a far more dreadful nature than has been represented."

"Doctor Charlton is in attendance upon my master, Miss," said Jane; " and had you not better see him first ?"

"No—no—" impatiently replied Ethelinde, and she hurried up the stairs towards her father's chamber, followed by Mrs. Rayborne.

The doctor, who had been apprised of their arrival, met them at the door, and gently prevented their entrance. He drew them into an ante-room, and there Ethelinde, overpowered by her apprehensions, sunk into a chair, and looked anxiously at the doctor, unable at the same time to utter a word.

"This is indeed a most unfortunate affair," said the doctor; "but compose yourself, my dear young lady, and let us hope for the best. All that skill and attention can do, shall be done for your excellent father."

"Oh, sir, for Heaven's sake, do not keep me in suspense. Tell me how he is;" ejaculated Ethelinde. "But I must see him immediately."

"No, Miss Ethelinde," said Doctor Charlton, "you had better not at present. Your father has received a severe wound in his head, and is at present insensible. But still I trust that he is not in a dangerous condition."

"Oh, God!" exclaimed our heroine, and completely overpowered by the dreadful fears which crowded upon her imagination, she immediately fainted.

Mr. Clarence had reached within a short distance of his mansion, deeply buried in the most painful thought, when his horse took fright at something in the road, and started off at a speed which the unfortunate gentleman was totally unable to restrain. He was unattended, and, therefore, no assistance could be rendered him. The consequence was that the affrighted animal coming in contact with something that was lying across the road, fell, and Mr. Clarence was precipitated with fearful violence over his head, and received such severe injury that he was immediately deprived of his senses.

In that state he was found by some labouring men, and conveyed with all possible despatch to his residence, where his medical adviser was promptly in attendance.

Mrs. Rayborne and Doctor Charlton exerted themselves to the utmost to restore Ethelinde, and when she did recover, her agitation was painful to behold. Mrs. Rayborne in vain endeavoured to tranquillize her feelings.

"I must see my poor father immediately," she ejaculated, "and judge myself of the nature of his injury. Oh, God! that such an accident should occur, and at such a time."

Doctor Charlton and Mrs. Rayborne saw that it was to no purpose their trying to persuade Ethelinde from seeing her father, and she, therefore, entered the chamber, accompanied by the doctor, and hastened to the bed-side with a hasty and anxious step.

Mr. Clarence was, as the doctor had stated, in a state of total unconsciousness, and the ghastly aspect of his countenance struck horror to the bosom of Ethelinde. She pressed her lips upon his cheek—she called upon his name, in a voice of the utmost emotion, and endeavoured to recall him to sensibility, and it was in vain that the worthy doctor sought to tranquillize her feelings by assuring her there was no immediate danger. She seated herself by the bed-side, at length, after having supplicated the mercy of Heaven, and nothing whatever could induce her to quit the chamber.

Mrs. Rayborne came into the room, and tried all she could to soothe her, and inspire her with hope, but with little success.

Mr. Clarence appeared to breathe freely, but the ghastly aspect of his countenance, and the totally inanimate state in which he laid, seemed to be the certain prelude to death; and when Ethelinde reflected upon the situation in which she would be placed, should death deprive her of her only earthly protector, her agony of mind may be readily conceived.

"Oh, merciful God!" she ejaculated, clasping her hands, and raising her eyes towards Heaven, "I beseech thee to avert that dreadful calamity, and whatever may be the fate to which thy divine will may have destined me, do not, oh, do not suffer me to experience so terrible a bereavement."

"That Almighty Being to whom you have appealed, my sweet girl," said Mrs. Rayborne, "depend on it, will not turn a deaf ear to your earnest and virtuous supplications. Our worthy friend here, Doctor Charlton, has declared it as his opinion that your amiable father is not in any immediate danger, and let us hope, with the blessing of God, and his skill, that he will ere long be restored to convalescence, and live many years to protect and love you."

"Oh, madam," sighed our heroine, pressing the hand of Mrs. Rayborne to her lips, "how kind it is of you thus to endeavour to console me in my affliction. Would to Heaven that I could encourage the same hopes which you profess, but alas! I cannot; a melancholy, a dreadful presentiment, has taken possession of my mind, which I find it utterly impossible to shake off.

"My dear young lady," said Doctor Charlton, "indeed you must not give way to this, or you will place your own life in peril. Again I assure you, as far as my own judgment dictates to me, that you have no immediate danger to apprehend. Your respected father has certainly received a severe injury in the head, but the symptoms he shows, up to the present moment, are favourable to him, and I feel little doubt, that, if he is not in any way excited, when he is restored to sensibility, all will go well. Pray retire, and endeavour to compose yourself, and depend upon it, I will give you timely notice should any unfavourable change take place."

"Aye, Ethelinde, my dear girl," said Mrs. Rayborne, warmly pressing her hand; "take Mr. Charlton's excellent advice, and for the present leave your poor father to his care and attention. Retire with me, my sweet girl, to another apartment, and I feel satisfied that, in a short time, you will receive the most favourable intelligence."

The expressive eyes of Ethelinde fully acknowledged the kindness of Mrs. Rayborne, but still she hesitated, for her anxiety was so great, that she had the greatest difficulty imaginable to leave her father, even for a moment. The arguments of the doctor and Mrs. Rayborne, however, at last prevailed, and she consented to retire with the latter, whilst Doctor Charlton should exert all his energies to restore his patient to sensibility.

Again she fixed her earnest gaze upon the countenance of her revered parent, and having kissed his venerable cheeks, she gave her arm to Mrs. Rayborne, and suffered her to lead her from the chamber.

When they were alone, Mrs. Rayborne exercised all the eloquence at her command to tranquilize the feelings of her beautiful young friend, but for some time she was completely inconsolable.

"Alas! alas!" sighed Ethelinde, "in spite of all that you say, my kind friend, and the reasonableness of the arguments you advance, I feel a sad foreboding that my dear father will never recover. Oh, what would then become of me?—How should I be able to protect myself against the evil machinations of Everard Welford? If he persecutes me now, what am I to expect when deprived of my natural protector?"

"For Heaven's sake, my dearest Ethelinde, do not give way to these gloomy thoughts," said Mrs. Rayborne; —"the Almighty is too merciful to place you in such a melancholy position. He will restore your father to health, and depend upon it all will yet be well."

"God grant that it may be as you predict, my dear madam," said our heroine, "but indeed I cannot bring my mind to think so. And then this horrible secret;—will it never be divulged to me?—"

Mrs. Rayborne scarcely knew what answer to make, and she found it was indeed a most difficult task to dissipate the melancholy impressions which had taken such strong hold of Ethelinde's mind.

Ethelinde frequently sent to inquire after the state of her father, but was informed that he remained in the same state of insensibility, although he breathed freely, and evinced no other alarming symptoms. The wound too, which he had received in the fall, exhibited no signs of inflammation, and the doctor augured from all appearances, that the present calm and unconscious state in which his patient was lying would be productive of the most favourable results.

Ethelinde did feel more reconciled by these appearances, and shortly afterwards Mrs. Rayborne was compelled to take her leave, and she was left to her own reflections.

As may be expected, they were of the most gloomy description, and many were the prayers she offered up to the Supreme Being for the restoration of her revered parent; fearful were the anticipations she entertained, should it be the will of Heaven to take him from her. Her heart sickened at the bare thought!

And now again the threats of Everard Welford recurred to her memory, and she shuddered at the contemplation of the difficulties by which she was on every side surrounded. She was perfectly convinced that Everard would not fail to prosecute his odious suit, let the consequences be whatever they might, and should she be left unprotected, what power had she of resisting him, unless she were to leave the neighbourhood altogether, and retire to some spot where he might be unable to discover her. But then whither could she go? What friend had she who could shield her from his advances? Mrs. Rayborne she knew would willingly do so, but she was not only completely powerless, but in some measure dependent on Mr. Welford and his son.

Unable any longer to remain from the chamber of her father, and to endure the agony of her own thoughts, Ethelinde arose and quitted the apartment, and once more sought the couch of the sufferer.

Mr. Clarence had undergone no change since she had left him. His countenance was pale and ghastly, but still he appeared to be in a calm sleep.

"Oh, that he would arouse from this dreadful state of torpor; would that I could once more hear the sound of his beloved voice;" she ejaculated.

"Be calm, my dear young lady, and wait patiently;" said doctor Charlton. "Your respected parent will doubtless be restored to consciousness anon, and much depends upon your being cool and collected on the occasion; for the least excitement which he might experience, would be almost certain to be productive of consequences of the most dangerous description."

"I will endeavour to act in accordance with your wishes, my dear sir," said Ethelinde, "but I am sure that you can make every allowance for my feelings on this occasion."

"Indeed, I do, Miss Ethelinde," replied the doctor, "and heartily do I hope that your apprehensions may prove to be groundless, as I feel all but convinced that they will."

"Oh, thank you, sir, for that assurance," exclaimed our heroine, the tears starting from her eyes, "it is indeed a relief to my mind. My dear father, what should I do without you, and especially under the present threatening and perilous circumstances?"

For more than two hours did Ethelinde continue to watch with the most indescribable anxiety, her father's restoration to consciousness. At length he heaved a deep sigh, and opening his eyes, stared vacantly around him.

"Father, beloved father," cried Ethelinde, in tones of anguish we need not attempt to describe; "I am here, your own child, your Ethelinde, is at your side. Speak to her, I implore you, and tell her how you are."

Mr. Clarence stared at his daughter wildly for a moment or two; returned no answer, and closing his eyes, once more relapsed into his former state of torpor.

"Alas! alas!" she groaned, and clasped her hands convulsively together, "he did not appear to recognize me. The injury he has received seems to have deprived him of his senses altogether. Oh, God, sustain me in this dreadful hour of trial."

"Do not alarm yourself, Miss," said Doctor Charlton, "I have every hope of your father's recovery."

It was a difficult matter, however, to at all quiet the fears, or to appease the anguish of Ethelinde. Her tears flowed fast, and the doctor remained silent, thinking it better not to interrupt the ebullition of her grief, and left her to indulge in her own reflections.

How anxiously did the poor girl continue to watch by her father's couch; with what torturing anxiety did she notice every change in his countenance, and, how eagerly did she look forward to some favourable symptom, which might indicate his recovery.

A dreary, a tedious watching was that same, but at length the intense feelings which pressed upon her mind, overpowered her, and she sank gradually into the same description of torpor that her father was then labouring under.

Doctor Charlton summoned the attendants, and our heroine was conveyed to her chamber.

CHAPTER V.

THE SECOND INVERVIEW BETWEEN EVERARD AND ETHELINDE.—THE MADNESS OF MAJOR CLARENCE.

IT was not long ere Everard Welford and his father were informed of the accident which had occurred to Mr. Clarence, and greatly did it alarm them, considering the interest they had at stake.

It was only by the intimidation of the major, and the *certain* power they possessed over him through one unfortunate circumstance of his life, that they could hope to gain the consummation of their ends. While he lived they could hold him in constant dread of exposure, and therefore secure the fulfillment of the oath they had extorted from him; but should he die, there would be an end to the advantage they had imagined themselves to have obtained. Our heroine might be terrified at the idea of the memory of her father being stigmatized, but still she would never yield to the persuasions of Everard in becoming his wife, and therefore all his hopes would be annihilated.

"Curses light upon this accident," Everard exclaimed, "it will retard, if not ultimately defeat the completion of my plans. And yet," he added, whilst a sardonic smile overspread his features, it might not be convenient to the fair but haughty Ethelinde Clarence, to hear her father denounced to the world as a criminal, as one who had forfeited his neck to the hangman;—who had been living upon sufferance, even though he no longer existed to pay the penalty. I hold the proofs, the indubitible proofs to substantiate the correctness of the accusation, and the world is illiberal enough to condemn and scout the irresponsible offspring of the guilty party. In that I feel my triumph, and the certainty that Ethelinde will sooner yield to my wishes than have obloquy cast upon her father's memory. By all my hopes, I would sooner sacrifice fortune, life, everything, then allow the beauteous Ethelinde to escape from becoming my bride."

Thus did Everard Welford soliloquize soon after he had received the intelligence of the accident which had occurred to Major Clarence. He was shortly joined by his father.

"The major is in a very dangerous condition;" said Mr. Welford.

"So I understand," answered his son.

"It would be a bad thing if he were to die, Everard," observed his father.

"It would," coincided the young man.

"While he lives," continued Mr. Welford, "we hold a supreme power over him, and the union between you and his daughter is certain. He has only a choice between that and certain disgrace, perhaps an ignominous death."

"True."

"But should he die."

"Ah, should he die,—how think you then, father?"

"Why—why—you I believe are pretty well satisfied that you do not possess the love of his daughter?"

"She has told me so."

"Well—well."

"The beggar Norman Rayborne, holds the sovereignty of her heart; he has gone far from his native land;—he may never return (may he be swallowed up in the green waves of the ocean long before he can reach the place of his destination). Ethelinde will be left without protectors, and it will be my fault if Ethelinde does not become my victim, in spite of all her obduracy. Father, I have set my mind upon the accomplishment of my wishes, and I flatter myself that I possess too much of your own spirit of determination to suffer myself to be defeated."

"Well said, my boy," observed Mr. Welford, grasping his son's hand, in a congratulatory manner. "You must, you shall succeed."

"I am fully determined that nothing short of death shall prevent me;" returned Everard.

"You must again see Ethelinde; and, by the bye, while her father is in his present dangerous situation, I think it would not be a bad opportunity of prosecuting your suit to advantage. In her present unsettled state of mind you might win from her a promise that no persuasion would tempt her to yield under other circumstances."

"An admirable suggestion, father,"

said Everard, "I will most assuredly avail myself of it. But still I hope that Major Clarence will not die."

"No, it would be rather inconvenient for him to do so, *for us* at present. While he lives he is in constant dread of us, and consequently gives us a power over his daughter."

"Very true."

"And then you know, Everard," continued Mr. Welford, "that Major Clarence is now immensely rich; he has a large portion to give to his daughter, and I am sorry to say from the extravagant way in which we have lived, and from other causes, such a dowry as he would be able to give with the fair Ethelinde, would be very convenient, to say the least of it."

"Ah!" ejaculated Everard, slightly biting his lips.

"A wealthy heiress, and a handsome, a beautiful woman, is worth straining a point to gain possession of, Everard."

"I am fully sensible of that;" remarked Everard, with a smile;—"and she shall be mine, or I will perish in the attempt to obtain possession of her."

"Bravely spoken, my boy, you will triumph, I know you will."

"I shall be much mistaken if I do not," returned Everard; "the more I see of the beauteous Ethelinde, in spite of the scorn, and almost hatred, she evinces towards me, the more do I love her. By Heaven! I would sooner suffer the most torturing death than to see her the bride of another. But I am all impatience until I behold her again."

"And yet it can hardly be expected that she will grant you an interview while her father is in his present dangerous situation."

"It is the time, as you have observed, when I can play upon her weakest points, and exact from her a promise which nothing can absolve her from. I am determined not to miss the opportunity which is presented to me."

"Well, well, I commend you for your boldness and resolution, my boy," said Mr Welford, "and I flatter myself that success will crown our designs. Should Major Clarence die, his daughter would not like his memory to be blasted with the crime of which we can accuse him, and of which we possess such unquestionable proofs, and therefore she is certain

to yield to your importunities; and though you at present possess not her love, as your bride, I have no doubt you will be able to work a change over her sentiments."

"But have you the papers secure?" demanded Everard, eagerly.

"Have I not shewn them you?" replied his father. "I have them all secure; and once revealed to the world, Major Clarence is blasted for ever."

"True, true," returned Everard; "I am satisfied. The power I possess over Ethelinde and her father, it is impossible for them to stand against."

"You are right, my boy," replied the old gentleman; "in spite of everything our triumph is certain; and let me only see you the husband of Ethelinde Clarence, I shall be the happiest man in existence."

Thus saying, Mr. Welford quitted the presence of his son, and left him to his own reflections.

The reader will have perceived from the slight portraiture which has been given of Mr. Welford, that he was a character of the most detestable kind. Mean, sordid, unprincipled, crafty, and designing, he only possessed sufficient cunning to carry out those objects; in every other respect he was superlatively ignorant.

Yet was Mr. Welford sufficiently ingenious to conceal his real character from the majority of those who came in contact with him, and he was almost universally esteemed as a man of probity and worth, while those who had some inkling of his real character, happened to be his own dependents, and were in consequence afraid to give utterance to their opinions.

His son, under the mask of every generous and noble feeling, possessed similar qualities to those of his father, with the exception of his ignorance, for Everard Welford was accomplished and intelligent, and his society was eagerly courted by the fashionables of the neighbourhood.

A tendency towards dissipation he had even from his earliest youth displayed, and that was, perhaps what more than all, prejudiced Ethelinde against him, and she had when she became older, shunned his society as much as possible, fearful that he might indulge in hopes which she could never, for a moment think of encouraging.

"Yes," exclaimed Everard, when his father had left him, "you need not fear that I will fail to prosecute my suit, and if I fail it shall not be from any fault of mine. Ethelinde, you may scorn me, despise me, hate me, but in spite of everything, you must, you shall be mine. You little imagine the power I hold over your destiny, and I will not fail to exercise it. Let your father live or die, you shall become my bride. Shall I ever suffer the beggar Norman Rayborne to carry off the prize I so much covet?— No,—I should hate, I should despise myself, could I think of such a sacrifice. But Norman has left his native land, he may never return, and should he do so, it will be to see his darling Ethelinde the bride of his hated rival. Oh, I anticipate a most glorious triumph, in spite of the obstinate opposition of her whom I have chosen to be my future partner."

He chuckled to himself as he gave utterance to these words, and paced the apartment two or three times hastily, rubbing his hands. And yet, under all the circumstances, he could not but deeply regret the accident which had befallen Major Clarence, for should he die, it might, notwithstanding all his efforts to the contrary, decrease his power over Ethelinde. She would seek the protection of friends, undoubtedly, and it would be useless for him to attempt to prosecute his suit, for she would be certain to resist him, in spite of his threats to reveal to the world the crime of which her father had been guilty. While he lived, on the contrary, she was in his absolute power, for, however, revolting to her feelings, she would sooner sacrifice her hand to him, than for a moment she could contemplate her father's character, nay, perhaps his life, being placed in jeopardy.

"However," he remarked, "I will not be daunted, but proceed with determination, and I fear not but that I shall triumph in the end. At any rate, I am resolved that if Ethelinde does not accept my hand she shall never become the bride of another man, especially Norman Rayborne. Oh, how I hate even the name of that man. Had Ethelinde never beheld him, I might have won her love, and all this anxiety,

this trouble, and vexation might have been spared me. Curses light upon him, and may some accident occur to prevent his ever returning to England."

Again did Everard traverse the apartment with hasty steps, devising plans to carry his wishes into effect, and alternately muttering curses to himself. But at length he sized his hat, and leaving the house directed his footsteps towards the mansion of the unfortunate Mr. Clarence.

Ethelinde was still keeping her melancholy watch in the chamber of her father. He had recovered from his state of torpor, but he knew her not, nor any one who appeared before him. His wound presented no other unfavourable symptoms, but oh, how great was the agony of his lovely daughter, as she called upon his name, and in vain endeavoured to rouse him to recollection. He only stared at her vacantly, and then muttered some incoherent sentences to himself. It was maddening to behold him in such a melancholy condition; and the worthy doctor found all his arguments of no avail in tranquillizing her feelings.

It was in the midst of this tribulation that Everard Welford arrived at the mansion, and sent up a message, requesting an interview with our heroine.

Ethelinde shuddered with a sensation nearly allied to horror, when she heard his name mentioned.

"Oh, I dare not, I will not see him," she ejaculated; "How entirely destitute of all feeling he must be, to request an interview at such a time as this. I pray you, my dear sir," she added, addressing Doctor Charlton, "to hasten to him and excuse me from meeting him."

"I will readily do so, my dear young lady," said the Doctor, "and in the meantime, I beg of you to endeavour to calm your feelings, for you have nothing to fear. Mr. Welford surely cannot, under the painful circumstances, urge his request."

Ethelinde shook her head, and sighed deeply, and Doctor Charlton quitted the chamber.

On entering the apartment where Everard was waiting, the latter turned upon the worthy Doctor a haughty look, which he met with perfect indifference.

"I requested to see Miss Clarence,"

said Everard, haughtily, "not Doctor Charlton."

"I presume sir," replied the doctor, "that your visit is merely one of condolence on account of the unfortunate accident which has befallen Major Clarence, and if such is the fact, I, on the part of Miss Ethelinde, beg leave to thank you for your sympathy and attention."

"I repeat, sir," said Everard, with a frown, "that my business is with Miss Clarence, and not with you."

"Miss Clarence is in the chamber of her father, and you surely cannot be so unreasonable as to expect that she can be in any state of mind to grant interviews at present."

"Am I to understand, sir," demanded Everard, "that Ethelinde Clarence refuses to see me?"

"She respectfully declines to do so on the present occasion, sir;" replied the doctor coolly;—"but if you have any message, I will deliver it."

"I must and will see her;" exclaimed Everard, losing all control over his temper.

"You cannot, Mr. Welford," returned Doctor Charlton, firmly, "and allow me to say that this language and conduct is very unbecoming, to say the least of it."

"That is your opinion, Doctor Charlton," said Everard, with a sneer.

"It is," answered the former, "and I will add that it inflicts no credit either upon the courtesy or humanity of the person who is guilty of it."

"Indeed!" said Everard, with a frown; "however, I came not here to bandy arguments with you, Doctor Charlton; but as you have undertaken to be the bearer of a message from me, I would thank you to inform Ethelinde, that I shall repeat my visit to-morrow, and that if she then refuses to see me, I will utter something aloud that will give her cause to tremble. Good day, Doctor Charlton."

And without saying another word, Everard stalked from the room, and quitted the house, leaving the worthy doctor overwhelmed with disgust and indignation.

The worthy doctor hesitated for a few moments, and deliberated upon what Everard had said. To him it seemed perfectly inexplicable, and yet it did not appear feasible that young Welford would hold out such threats and insinuations, unless there was some means in his power to carry them out, and to corroberate them if necessary.

Mr. Charlton was lost in perplexity. He deeply sympathised with Major Clarence and his amiable and lovely daughter in their peculiar situation, and entertained the best of wishes towards them both, but still he was most anxious to be informed by what means it was that Everard Welford and his father exercised the power, which from the observations of the former, they did over Mr. Clarence and his daughter.

The brutal and insolent conduct of Everard he could never sufficiently condemn, and he was fully determined, if anything lay in his power so to do, to frustrate his views, which he was satisfied were of the most diabolical description.

But he scarcely knew how to impart to our heroine the result of his interview with Everard in her present distressed state of mind. The manner of Everard convinced him that he knew he held a certain power over Ethelinde and her father which she could not resist, and that she therefore, dare not disobey his command.

It caused the worthy doctor some serious reflection, as we have said before, ere he could return to the chamber of the invalid, and when he did so, he found Ethelinde most anxiously awaiting him. Mr. Clarence was in the same state in which the doctor had left him, aroused from his state of torpor, but gazing with a wild and vacant stare upon his daughter, and around the apartment, which impressed the mind of Mr. Charlton with the most alarming apprehensions as to the final result of his illness, and the malady under which he was labouring.

"Has Mr. Welford gone?" eagerly inquired Ethelinde."

"He has," answered Doctor Charlton.

"Oh, thank Heaven!" fervently ejaculated our heroine; "then he has the good sense and humanity to act with forbearance?"

The Doctor shook his head, significantly, and Ethelinde looked anxiously at him for an explanation.

"Did he appear vexed at my declining to see him?" demanded Ethelinde.

The doctor answered in the affirmative.

"And did he say when he would call again ?" asked our heroine.

"To-morrow, miss ;" replied Mr. Charlton.

"To-morrow !"

"Yes," and the doctor added in an under tone and looking round upon his patient ;—"he further said that, if you refused to see him you would have cause to repent it."

"Oh, God ! oh, God !" groaned Ethelinde, clasping her hands, "my worst

MR. CLARENCE IS THROWN FROM HIS HORSE.

fears are realized ; what shall protect me from his inhumanity !"

Doctor Charlton endeavoured to console her, while her unfortunate father looked on, perfectly unconscious, and with the air of a maniac.

"Oh, how can I evade the dark ma-

chinations he has against me ?" said Ethelinde. "Villain that he must be to persist, knowing the misery of my present situation, the calamity which has so unexpectedly fallen upon me."

"Ah, my dear young lady," said the doctor, "if the Welfords possess the power over you and your father, which Everard boasts they do, I fear that you have little to hope from their clemency."

"I cannot see him!" sighed our heroine.

"The interview, no doubt, will be a most agonising and insulting one to your feelings, Miss Ethelinde," observed Doctor Charlton, "but still I would advise you to endeavour to muster courage to meet him."

"And my poor father, too, in this melancholy condition;" groaned our heroine, and her tears at the same time flowed copiously;—"See, how vacantly he gazes upon me, and is entirely unconscious of everything that is passing around him. Oh, I shall go mad!"

"Pray be calm, my dear young lady," said the good doctor, "and put your trust in that all merciful Providence, who, no doubt, will bring you safely through all the dangers with which you are at present threatened."

"What have I done,—what has my father done, that we should be thus cruelly persecuted?" said Ethelinde.

"Bear with it patiently, my poor girl," said Mr. Charlton, in his most compassionate accents.

"Alas! alas! would to Heaven that I could," Ethelinde replied. "But when I reflect upon all that Everard Welford has said to me, my heart trembles with terror."

"But, Miss Clarence," remarked the doctor, "you surely are not dependent upon him, and while your father remains in his present condition I will undertake to protect you from his persecutions."

"Oh, my dear sir," returned Ethelinde, "how can I sufficiently thank you for your kindness? But, alas! I fear that all your good intentions will be of little or no avail. Everard Welford and his father possess a certain power over me and my unfortunate father, which is almost as inscrutable to me as yourself, and the nature of which I dare not name. Would to God that he could be persuaded to postpone his interview with me for the present at any rate."

"You may rest assured, my dear young lady," replied the doctor, "that I did all in my power to induce him to relent, but it was all to no purpose."

"I am much obliged to you for all your services, Mr. Charlton," observed Ethelinde; "and I am certain that you can feel for the painful and delicate situation in which I am placed."

"Indeed I do, Miss," replied the doctor, "and nothing would afford me greater pleasure than to be able to release you from it. As for your poor father, notwithstanding his present melancholy symptoms, I am not without the most sanguine hopes, I assure you, of his ultimate recovery,"

"Oh, thank you for that assurance, and may Heaven grant that your expectations may be verified. But what said Everard Welford? Pray tell me all; do not conceal anything from me;—I am ready to hear it, and knowing it shall be better prepared to meet him, and to combat his odious importunities."

"Mr. Charlton complied and stated the particulars of his interview, in an undertone of voice, to which Ethelinde listened with the most profound attention, and in a state of the greatest agitation of mind imaginable.

That Everard should persist in demanding an interview with her, knowing the dangerous situation in which her father was placed, and the consequent agitation of mind she must be enduring, convinced her; if any thing had been wanting that he was entirely destitute of all manly or proper feeling, at the same time it showed her, how little she had to expect from his mercy and forbearance.

She beat her breast in despair, and was entirely deaf to all the efforts at consolation which the worthy Doctor Charlton offered. She saw plainly enough that she had no other alternative than to meet Everard Welford the following day, he seemed determined to take every cowardly advantage, and what the result of that interview might be, she shuddered even to think upon.

Throughout the day Mr. Clarence continued in much the same state. Sometimes, he appeared to have recovered slightly to consciousness, and would call upon his daughter's name, but when she threw her fair arms around his neck, and implored him to speak to her, he would quickly relapsed into his former state of half idiotcy, laugh wildly, and turn away from her as if she were a stranger or something loathsome. Need we say how this wrung the poor girl's heart? Many were the tears she shed, and deep was the despair which gradually settled upon her, and which not all the kind remonstrances of Doctor Charlton could remove.

In the course of the day Ethelinde was visited by Kate Rayborne and her mother, and to them she unfolded all her thoughts without reserve, and made them acquainted with what had taken place at the recent interview between Doctor Charlton and Everard Welford.

Nothing could exceed the disgust and indignation which Mrs. Rayborne and her daughter evinced, at conduct so inhuman, so insolent, and so overbearing; but they exerted themselves to the utmost to cheer the spirits of Ethelinde, and to inspire her with the hope that she would yet triumph over the evil machinations of her persecutor.

It was a difficult task however, to induce Ethelinde to think anything of the kind; she felt too keenly, after what had passed, the secret power which Everard Welford and his father held over her and her unfortunate parent, and she saw nothing but misery before her.

It was not till late in the evening that Mrs. Rayborne and Kate took their leave, and they then did so with the deepest regret, for they saw how much Ethelinae needed their consolation and advice; but they promised to see her again on the following day, and trusted that the result of the meeting between her and Everard Welford, would be much better than she at present anticipated.

Ethelinde shook her head, but made no reply, and Kate and her mother having departed, she once more returned to the chamber of her suffering father, and resumed her weary and anxious watching.

And in good truth, a dreary and anxious watching it was, and heavily did the anguish of Ethelinde increase, and she turned a deaf ear to all the supplications of Doctor Charlton, (who was fearful that her constitution would sink under so much fatigue) to retire to rest.

Her father slept soundly, and calmly, and again Dr. Charlton prognosticated a favourable change; but still nothing could revive the spirits of Ethelinde, nor arouse within her one spark of hope.

She thought upon the coming morrow with feelings of the utmost dread. How could she meet Everard Welford in her present state of mind, and after the daring threats which he had held out? The bare idea was most revolting to her feelings, and the longer she reflected on it, the greater did her anguish and her fears increase.

Oh, God! how utterly insensible to every feeling of pity must Everard Welford be to persist in his odious suit under such circumstances. And what could she anticipate from such a man,—if he possessed the power of which he boasted, and which she had too much reason to believe was no exaggeration, —but the worst? It would be vain for her to attempt to resist him, for according to what he had said, and her unfortunate father by his prior statement to her hinted at, should the latter recover even from his present malady, his life was in Mr. Welford and his son's hands. What could could be the nature of that dreadful secret? How anxious was she, yet how she dreaded, at the same time, to become acquainted with it. The words of her father, and those of Everard, still rung in her ears; she could not shut them out, try all she could. They fell like a withering blight upon all her faculties, and almost overpowered her with their deadly influence.

How awful was this state of suspense to endure! Yet where could she look for consolation? How combat the fate with which she was threatened? It was dreadful to think upon, and yet she had no means of the least consolation or hope.

But surely Everard would not persist in demanding the interview with her on the following day, when he heard of the danger of her father, and knew the consequent anguish of mind she must be enduring. Callous and unfeeling as she had now so much reason to believe him, she could not think him so entirely destitute of every spark of humanity as to urge his suit under such trying circumstances.

Ethelinde continued by the side of her father's couch during the whole of that night, and watched him with the most indescribable anxiety. He slept calmly, and she began to hope for the most favourable results from this circumstance.

Incessant were the prayers she offered up to the fountain of all good, for his speedy recovery, and that he might be protected from the evil designs of his enemies.

That he could ever have been so guilty as had been so darkly hinted at both by himself and Everard Welford, she could not bring her mind to believe; and she endeavoured to flatter herself with the hope that all would yet be satisfactorily explained, and that the hopes of Everard would be disappointed, and his plans defeated; but to think of being compelled to become the wife of one whom she now so thoroughly hated, she could not without a shudder of horror. She would rather that a premature grave should close over her, than that she should be consigned to such a fate.

Still what alternative was left her, if her father's honour, name, nay, even his life, that life so precious to her, depended on it? She felt that even though her heart should break, which most assuredly it would, she must make the sacrifice.

And oh, what would be the anguish of her beloved Norman, did he but know the sufferings, the horrible fear and suspense she was now enduring; the peculiar, the extraordinary dilemma in which she was placed? It was indeed fortunate that he did not, for knowing that he was separated far away from her, and without the least means, if even he had been at home, of extricating her from the cruel fate with which she was threatened, would drive him to madness.

"Poor Norman," Ethelinde muttered to herself, while her heart throbbed with the most intense and indescribable anguish, "We shall never—we must never meet again. Cruel fate has conspired against us. But oh, may every happiness attend you, and may Heaven give you fortitude to support the disappointment of your hopes. As for me, alas! alas! I dare not anticipate the horrors which are in store for me."

Fast flowed the beauteous damsel's tears as these melancholy thoughts suggested themselves to her, and she gave herself up entirely to the agony of her feelings.

Ethelinde had resolutely resisted every persuasion to retire to her chamber, but towards the morning her strength was completely exhausted, and sleep overpowered her senses. But even then the most frightful dreams tortured her imagination, and the events of the last day or two were re-enacted in an exaggerated form.

She was suddenly aroused from this disturbed and unrefreshing slumber by hearing a loud and frenzied cry, and opening her eyes, she beheld her father sitting upright in the bed, supported by the doctor, and gazing madly around him. She started immediately towards him, and was about to throw her arms affectionately round his neck, when the doctor gently interposed, and by a significant look persuaded her to withdraw a little aside while he endeavoured to deal with his unfortunate patient.

"Father! dear, dear father!" cried Ethelinde, as she complied with Doctor Charlton's persuasions,—"Oh, speak to your poor girl, let me once more hear you repeat my name, and oh, how great will be the relief it will afford my mind."

The doctor shook his head; and Mr. Clarence stared vacantly at his distracted daughter for a moment or two, and then laughed idiotically. Ethelinde clasped her forehead in despair.

"Oh, God!" she exclaimed, "my poor father's reason has fled; it has fled for ever."

Mr. Charlton by a look sought to tranquillize her feelings, and fain would he have prevailed upon her to retire, and endeavour to regain her fortitude, but she sank again in her chair, and covering her face with her hands, sobbed bitterly, in fact, she gave the most unrestrained indulgence to the feelings which agonized her bosom.

Once more she looked up, and found her father in the same state in which she had seen him on awaking. He was laughing hysterically, and the wild, the maddening expression of his eyes were quite torturing to look upon.

"My dear young lady," said the doctor, "I beg of you to retire from the chamber, for while you are present you are not only endangering your own constitution, but preventing me from attending to your father as I ought to do. I trust that this will prove only a temporary paroxysm. Will you, Miss Clarence, accede to my advice, which I believe I need not add, has its source entirely in the best of motives."

"Oh, indeed I know that, my good, sir," replied our heroine, her earnest feelings of gratitude shining through her tears. "But I am confident that you can duly appreciate my feelings, and enter into the anguish of my thought, on seeing my poor father in this deplorable condition."

"Indeed I do, Miss Ethelinde," replied Doctor Charlton, "but, at the same time, you must, I know, fully admit the justice of the counsel I have given you, and not only for your own sake, but that of your amiable parent, will follow it. In a short time, I sincerely hope, your father will be sufficiently recovered for you to be readmitted to his presence, in the meanwhile, I beg of you to retire, and try to revive your spirits, and to put your trust in that great, that omnipotent power, which never deserts the good and the virtuous in their time of need,"

Ethelinde pressed the hand of the worthy doctor to her lips, but her heart was too full to allow her to speak. She felt the full force and reason of Mr. Charlton's arguments, and was determined, notwithstanding it would cause a severe struggle to her feelings, to yield to them. She approached her suffering parent. She threw her fair arms around his neck, she called affectionately upon his name, and endeavoured, but in vain to arouse him to recollection. He only stared vacantly at her, as he had previously done. It was quite evident from the wildness of his eyes, and the general expression of his countenance, that the ill-fated gentleman's reason had fled. He did not recognise her, his only, his darling child; and with a burst of the most indescribable anguish she withdrew herself from his embrace, and retired from the room.

On reaching her own apartment, she sunk into a chair, and there gave unrestrained indulgence to the agonising feelings which beset her mind in a copious flood of tears. It seemed as though all the miseries of her fate were concentrated in that one moment of intense suffering. All the maddening prospects of the future rushed upon her fevered brain with overwhelming influence. She saw nothing but ruin and torture before

her, and ardently did she wish that the Almighty would deprive her of life, rather than suffer her to live to experience such cruelty, persecution, and probably shame and degradation.

If her poor father survived his present unfortunate accident, it seemed but too probable from the symptoms he at present evinced, that his reason was gone for ever, and what hope was there left for her, if she should be thus deprived of his protection and friendly advice. The bare contemplation was terrible, and poor Ethelinde turned from it with a shudder. Alas! she asked herself, what had either she or her parent done, that they should be thus severely visited?

True, her father had been accused, he had accused himself of having been guilty of some desperate crime, by which his life was even forfeited to the offended laws of his country. But could she believe it? Oh, no! Nature, reason, every feeling revolted from the encouragement of such a thought. It was impossible! Her father must be labouring under some extraordinary, some fearful delusion. And yet why should he entertain such an evident dread of the power which he acknowledged that Mr. Welford and his son held over him? That, at any rate, went a long way to prove that there was some truth in what had been asserted, and in spite of all her efforts to the contrary, the anguish of Ethelinde arose to the most insupportable degree.

And this was the day too, that Everard Welford had threatened once more to visit her, and on which he demanded an interview, or in case of a refusal, held out an intimidation the nature of which she shuddered to think upon. But surely he could not be so cruel as to persist in doing so, knowing her own melancholy situation, and the almost hopeless condition of her father? He would certainly bethink himself, and act with more forbearance, for how could he ever hope to inspire her with any other feelings than those of terror and disgust by conduct so diametrically opposite to every manly generous, and honourable principle.

And even should Everard make his threatened visit, could she see him? It was utterly impossible for her to do so, in her present state of mind, let the consequences be whatever they might. She felt that she must sink entirely over-powered in his presence.

Frequently did Ethelinde send Jane to inquire after her father, but she was distracted to learn that he exhibited no more favourable symptoms, but the doctor begged that she would not return to the chamber, for the present, at any rate, as it might have the most dangerous effect upon her spirits, without operating in the least way beneficially to the invalid.

Ethelinde reluctantly complied with this request, but the suffering it cost her to do so, may be readily imagined. Much to her relief, shortly afterwards Kate Rayborne and her mother were announced and were immediately ushered into her presence. They were much grieved to find her in the deplorable state of anguish that she was, but still it was no more than they had expected under all the circumstances, and still more deeply did they regret when they heard from her the melancholy condition of her father. Mrs. Rayborne, however, did all that she could to soothe her under her severe affliction, although she scarcely knew what argument to make use of which was at all calculated to inspire her with hope.

"Alarming as his present symptoms appear, my dear Ethelinde," she remarked, "you must not yet give way to despair. The all-merciful God will not suffer you to experience so dreadful a bereavement as the loss of so excellent a parent, and dismal as I must admit your prospects at present are, the clouds which at present overcast your view will speedily pass away, and all will again be sunshine and happiness."

"Oh, that I could encourage such an idea," said our heroine, "but, alas! I cannot, and indeed I fear, my dear madam that your hopes are too sanguine. My poor father's reason has fled, and even should he survive, I fear that he will never recover it. My God! my God! how little was I prepared for such an affliction, such an awful calamity as this."

"Pray dear Ethelinde," said Kate, in her tenderest, her most sympathising accents, "endeavour not to yield entirely to this terrible despair. Even in the midst of our severest trials Omnipotence has the power to raise us to the very pinnacle of happiness, and most sincerely, most fervently do I hope that such may be the case with you."

Ethelinde took her fair friend's hand, and looked affectionately through her tears in her countenance, as she replied :—

"I know you do, my sweet Kate, but I cannot, indeed I cannot, notwithstanding, Heaven knows, I have struggled hard to do so, give way to any such hopes, which I have too much reason to apprehend would prove to be fallacious."

"Would that I could banish such dismal ideas from your mind, Ethelinde," said Mrs. Rayborne.

"Your father's unfortunate malady entirely arises from the nature of the injury he has received, and I trust that it will be only temporary. Mr. Charlton you know possesses the most eminent skill, and he has expressed the most sanguine hopes of his recovery."

"True, madam," answered Ethelinde, "but still in spite of all his exertions and good wishes, he may be disappointed. Alas! I see myself surrounded with the most terrible dangers, and have too much reason to fear that my troubles are only begun. The inexorable and insolent conduct of Everard Welford inspires me with an unconquerable feeling of terror. The dark hints he has thrown out, and the assertions of my poor father, convince me that he possesses a certain mysterious power over me, which he has determined to exercise to the fullest extent."

"He will not, he surely cannot go to extremes;" remarked Mrs. Rayborne.

"What else can I expect, my dear madam?" demanded our heroine, "after what he has said. And I am now thoroughly convinced that Everard Welford is not the sort of man to be moved from any purpose upon which he has fixed his mind. I cannot now think of him with any other feelings than those of dread and repugnance."

"I still cannot help thinking," said Mrs. Rayborne, "that Everard Welford, will see through the cruelty and injustice of his conduct, and act with more forbearance."

"To-day he comes again to the mansion," said Ethelinde, "and has commanded me to meet him, and to listen, no doubt, to his odious importunities, or has threatened that I shall have reason most bitterly to repent it."

"It is impossible surely that he can be so utterly destitute of every feeling of humanity and decency as to persist in that presumptuous determination. He will abandon such a design, and for the present, at any rate, defer the prosecution of his suit."

"There is no hope of it, madam," replied our heroine, "I cannot for a moment entertain it; and, oh, how can I find courage to meet him, tortured as my mind at present is? God of Heaven! teach me how to act, for I am completely distracted and bewildered."

Again both Mrs. Rayborne and her lovely daughter, used all their exertions to compose her, but with little or no effect; although she did feel a little consolation when she received a message from the worthy doctor, informing her that her father had become more tranquil, and seemed likely to sink off to sleep again; but still he advised her not to visit the chamber again for the present, but to endeavour to recruit her strength, hoping as he did that a few hours would produce a still more favourable change in his patient, when she could see him without danger.

"There," ejaculated Mrs. Rayborne, eagerly, "did I not tell you, my sweet Ethelinde, that Providence often raises us in the very midst of our despair to the summit of happiness? Mr. Charlton is not the man to endeavour to inspire you with false hopes, and depend upon it he sees good reason to expect a speedy and favourable change in your respected father, or he would not have ventured such a statement."

"Heaven send that it may turn out as Mr. Charlton has predicted," fervently exclaimed Ethelinde; "but I must confess that, in spite of everything, I still have my most fearful doubts."

Mrs. Rayborne was about to make a reply, when she was interrupted by a knock at the room door, and Jane entered, and informed our alarmed and deeply agitated heroine that Everard Welford was waiting below, and requested to see her.

Ethelinde turned ghastly pale, and trembled so violently that had she not caught the arm of Mrs. Rayborne she must have sunk insensible on the floor.

"Oh, God! What shall I do?" she cried; "I cannot see him. I cannot—I dare not listen to his hateful addresses in my present state of mind. Alas! how insensible to pity or shame must he be, thus to persist in urging his suit at a moment of affliction such as this. Oh, madam, advise me, tell me how to act?"

Mrs. Rayborne embraced her tenderly, and did all in her power to re-assure her.

"Be calm, Ethelinde," she observed; "and this adventure may terminate much better than you expect. Remain here with Kate, and I will see Mr. Welford, and try to expostulate with him. He surely cannot be entirely deaf to the voice of reason."

"Oh, thanks, thanks, my best friend," cried our heroine gratefully; "I know you will exert all your eloquence with Everard, and certainly he must be quite insensible to every manly and proper feeling, if you do not prevail over his wishes. Tell him that at some future time I will grant him the interview he now seeks; that I—but you know my mind; you know what I would say."

"Leave everything to me, my dear girl;" returned Mrs. Rayborne, "nothing shall be wanting on my part to accomplish all you wish."

Again did Ethelinde pour forth her thanks, and Mrs. Rayborne quitted the room, leaving our heroine and her youthful companion in a state of the greatest suspense as to what would be the result of her interview with Everard.

But when Ethelinde reflected that Mrs. Rayborne was the mother of his rival, she saw little or no reason to hope that her efforts would be crowned with any success, and she formed a pretty shrewd idea of the reception she was likely to meet with from him.

In the meantime Mrs. Rayborne made her way to the room in which Everard was waiting, fully resolved to do all that argument could effect to persuade him to desist, for the present at least, from his importunities, but with some misgivings herself as to the success she was likely to meet with.

On her entrance into the apartment, Everard's back was towards her, but hearing her footsteps, he hastily turned round, and on beholding who it was, he started back a pace or two, and a frown of anger and disappointment passed over his features.

Mrs. Rayborne, not at all abashed, advanced towards him, and curtseyed politely.

"To what am I indebted for the honour of this unexpected meeting, madam?" he demanded in sarcastic stones.

"Mr. Welford," replied Mrs. Rayborne, "pardon me if I appear intrusive but I wish to have a few words with you on the subject which I understand has brought you hither."

"Indeed," said Everard proudly, this certainly is most extraordinary, to say the least of it. Excuse me, Mrs. Rayborne, but the business which brings me here this morning cannot possibly concern you, and I must therefore decline to enter into any conversation upon it. I requested to see Miss Clarence, and I did not expect that she would again have ventured to refuse me."

"Mr. Welford," returned Mrs. Rayborne, not at all daunted by his coldness, "you must, I should think, naturally suppose that under all the circumstances Miss Clarence is in no state of mind to see visitors, and on her part, I beg that you will not urge her to see you until a more fitting opportunity."

"Everard bit his lips, and remained silent for a moment or two, during which interval he eyed Mrs. Rayborne with no friendly expression of countenance.

"Mrs. Rayborne," he said, at length, "I need not, I presume, remind you that my business is with Miss Clarence, and that I do not feel disposed, knowing the certain position you held as regards my interest, to receive you as an intercessor. You will perhaps pardon me for being so candid, but I must say that if Ethelinde has selected you for the office her choice has been a very ill-advised one, without for one moment, madam, (seeing that Mrs. Rayborne's indignation was aroused) attempting to detract from the perfect honesty and good feeling with which you have undertaken the task. But, at the same time Mrs. Rayborne, allow me to add, and it may perhaps be as well, and save a vast deal of unnecessary trouble that the explanation should be entered into at the present time, that Miss Clarence is affianced to me, has been from the earliest days of childhood, bound to me by a solemn pledge made

between our parents, which let Mr. Clarence break at his peril; I love her, and am determined not to resign my claim upon her hand to any man, especially Norman Rayborne."

"Norman Rayborne," retorted Mrs. Rayborne, proudly, and fixing upon her companion a look of supreme contempt, which he could not witness without some confusion, "is not here to defend his own pretensions, but his mother is, and thus she replies to you, Everard Welford; from Ethelinde's lips I have heard that although her hand may have been pledged to you, her heart is plighted to my son, and that nothing whatever shall induce her to break the solemn vows that have been made between them."

A sardonic grin passed over the features of Everard Welford as he listened to this, and it was evident from the general expression of his countenance that he exulted in some secret triumph.

"Indeed, madam," he said, with a bitter sneer, "but perhaps you will allow me to intimate to you that Ethelinde Clarence has only two alternatives, namely, to abandon all idea of your son, and to accept me as her husband, or should her father recover, to bring him to the gallows!"

"Oh, monstrous libel!" exclaimed Mrs. Rayborne. "It cannot be so. You take advantage of the present insensiblity of Major Clarence to hold out such an intimidation."

"Mrs. Rayborne," returned Everard, "I came not here to bandy words with you, but to demand an interview with Ethelinde. You have presumed to doubt my assertions, will she dare to put me to the test?"

"Oh, Mr. Welford," said Mrs. Rayborne, alarmed by the confidence and determination of his manner, "surely you cannot be so insensible to every proper feeling of delicacy and humanity. If you really bear the sentiments of affection towards Miss Clarence, that you profess to do, you will, especially under the circumstances of affliction in which she is at present placed, act with forbearance, and postpone your interview with her until another and more fitting occasion."

"This is trifling with me, madam," replied Everard, haughtily, "and I must, therefore, be candid and tell you that unless I see Ethelinde Clarence before I leave this house, I will say that which shall place the officers of justice in the sick chamber of her father."

Mrs. Rayborne looked at him for a moment or two, with mingled feelings of horror, astonishment, and disgust, and then replied,—

"Everard Welford," she said, "however much you may feel to triumph now, depend upon it the time *will* come when you will bitterly repent this. Your language is disgraceful to you as a man and a gentleman, it is base, cowardly, mean, and tyrannical, and——"

"Stop, stop, my good lady, who are so

THE VISIT OF EVERARD WELFORD ANNOUNCED TO ETHELINDE.

eloquent in your abuse;"—coolly and sarcastically interrupted Everard, "you seem to forget that your very amiable son is not present to defend the highly flattering opinion you seem to entertain of me, and in his absence I decline to listen any longer to your invectives. I repeat, that my business is with Ethelinde Clarence, and if you will so far oblige me by delivering to her the message, I have requested you to do, if she obstinately refuses, the consequences will be on her own head."

Mrs. Rayborne looked at him reproachfully and supplicatingly, but she saw plainly enough that he was determined, and that all efforts to move him to relent would be completely ineffectual. It grieved the worthy lady much to see her young friend placed in so awkward and delicate a position, and nothing could equal the indignation she felt at the unmanly and haughty conduct of Everard Welford. Her will was good enough to rebuke him severely, but fearful of what the consequences might be to Ethelinde, she restrained her feelings as well as she could, and resolved once more to try what effect persuasion would have upon Everard Welford.

"Mr. Welford," she observed, after a pause, during which interval the thoughts we have alluded to were passing in her mind, "I cannot believe you capable of such inhumanity as to attempt to carry out the threats you have made use of, especially against that amiable and afflicted girl towards whom you profess sentiments of love. Allow me to give it as my humble opinion that, to say the least of it, it is a most extraordinary way of showing the sincerity of your attachment, and certainly by no means calculated to conciliate the esteem of the object towards whom your importunities are directed. The critical situation of Mr. Clarence has naturally ——"

"This is trifling, madam," again interrupted Everard, haughtily, and he added, in a still more authoritative tone, "I repeat that my business is with Miss Clarence; she doubtless received the message which I delivered to Doctor Charlton yesterday, and it rests with her to decide whether she will grant me the interview I demand, or risk an exposure which will blast her happiness for ever."

Mrs. Rayborne looked at him with astonishment, disgust, and the bitterest reproach; but Everard met her glances with the most perfect indifference and contempt, which showed that he was fully determined to persist in his demands. The dark insinuations he had thrown out had both surprised and alarmed Mrs. Rayborne, and she was completely bewildered upon the subject, and knew not what to say for a few minutes, during which time, it was quite evident that the impatience of Everard was increasing to an almost insupportable degree, and that he was preparing himself for a burst of passion, which

Mrs. Rayborne was in no condition of mind to meet.

"I see, sir," she said at length, "that you have come here determined to turn a deaf ear to the voice of reason, and that it is useless therefore to appeal to you for forbearance. Surely common humanity might prompt you to a different course, and induce you to defer your interview to a more fitting occasion, and until Major Clarence shall be sufficiently recovered to afford his daughter the benefit of his advice and judgment."

"Am I again to remind you, Mrs. Rayborne," replied Everard, "that I am the master of my own actions, and that I am also prepared to take the responsibility of my conduct on myself? That Miss Clarence may be indisposed I do not doubt, but the nature of my business with her will admit of no delay, and I am determined to see her before I leave this house. As you have imposed upon yourself the task of becoming her intercessor, perhaps you will further condescend to deliver this message to her, and that without any farther unnecessary delay."

The insolent bearing of Everard was almost more than the mortified pride and indignation of Mrs. Rayborne could tamely submit to, and she had the greatest difficulty to control her feelings; but she saw at once that any expression of resentment would tend to no beneficial purpose, and she therefore restrained herself as much as possible.

"I will deliver your preremptory message to Miss Clarence," she said; "at the same time allow me to return you my acknowledgements for the particularly gentlemanly, and courteous manner in which you have conducted yourself on the present occasion towards myself. It cannot fail to leave the most favourable impression upon my mind as to the very estimable qualities, the extreme gallantry, and good sense of Mr. Everard Welford." As Mrs. Rayborne gave utterance to these words, she fixed upon Everard a look of the most bitter sarcasm, reproach, and contempt, and then, without waiting for any reply from him, she abruptly quitted the room, and with the most dismal forebodings she made her way to the apartment in which she had left Ethelinde and Kate.

Kate had exerted herself to the utmost, in the meantime, to compose the deeply agitated feelings of her fair friend, and to abate the fears which beset her mind, and her efforts were not altogether without success. The length of time that Mrs. Rayborne had been absent from the room, satisfied her that she was exerting all her powers of persuasion, and inspired her with the hope that Everard Welford would be prevailed upon to leave the mansion, without persisting in demanding an interview which she was in so unfit a state to encounter. But the looks of Mrs. Rayborne, on her return to the apartment, convinced her that these hopes were futile, and a cold shuddering ran through her frame, which nearly overpowered her entirely.

"My dear, madam," she eagerly ejaculated, "what success?"

Mrs. Rayborne shook her head, but taking the hand of our heroine in her's she endeavoured by one of her kindest and most sympathising looks to tranquillize her feelings.

"Oh, my kind friend," said Ethelinde, "surely Everard Welford, under the present melancholy circumstances, could not be so unfeeling as to refuse to listen to the voice of reason and friendly supplication?"

"Alas, my dear girl," replied Mrs. Rayborne, it grieves me to say that Everard is entirely insensible to all those generous and proper feelings—feelings which common humanity, delicacy, and gallantry should prompt. He has grossly insulted me likewise, and convinced me that he possesses a character of the most detestable description."

"Oh, Mrs. Rayborne," gushed forth Ethelinde, "how you shook my ears. But shall I not be spared this revolting meeting? Oh, tell me, Everard is gone, is he not?"

"No, Ethelinde," answered Mrs. Rayborne, "I could not prevail upon him to postpone the interview. He is still below, and insists upon seeing you."

"Oh, God," sighed our heroine, "is it possible that any man can be so cruel? But I dare not, cannot, will not see him."

"Pray, my dear Ethelinde," said Mrs. Rayborne, "do not agitate yourself thus severely. It is a severe trial I know but Providence will give you strength to support it, and from what Everard said that the consequences of your refusal would be most disagreeable."

"Oh, what did he say," eagerly demanded Ethelinde, "tell me all, I beseech you, that I may be prepared for the worst."

Mrs. Rayborne was about to comply with her request, as briefly as possible, when Jane again made her appearance with a peremptory message from Everard to the effect that he was determined not to await any longer, and that if Ethelinde did not immediately meet him, she must abide by what would most assuredly follow.

Ethelinde sunk, pale and terrified, into the arms of Mrs. Rayborne, and for a second or two was completely incapable of uttering a syllable.

"Good God!" she ejaculated at last; "teach me how to act. I can never find strength sufficient to encounter the terrors of this dreaded meeting. What can Everard Welford have to say, that he should seek so melancholy a time to communicate it? Oh, my poor father, what a terrible calamity it is that deprives me of your protection when I so much need it!"

"Cheer up, cheer up, Ethelinde," said Mrs. Rayborne, "and by your conduct on this occasion, show to Everard that you have resolution enough to set his insolent, unjust, and tyrannical designs at defiance. In spite of all his boasting and his threats, I feel satisfied that you may yet, if you act with firmness, triumph over him. The meeting, however painful to you, will soon be over, and I see no means of avoiding it. Come, I will attend you to the apartment in which Mr. Welford is waiting, and if possible remain with you until the interview is over."

"Oh, madam," said Ethelinde, "how can I ever sufficiently repay you for this kindness? I will brave the meeting, if only for my poor father's sake, for much I fear that the power which Everard states that he and his father hold over my unfortunate parent is not mere empty boasting."

She leant on the arm of Mrs. Rayborne, who gently led her trembling footsteps from the room, and assisted her in descending the stairs.

When they reached the door of the apartment in which Everard was waiting, they could hear him pacing backwards and forwards in the most excited manner, and muttering incoherent sentences to himself. Here Ethelinde was obliged to pause, and her fortitude almost entirely forsook her. Mrs. Rayborne whispered some words of encouragement and consolation in her ear, and she revived. Mrs. Rayborne then gently opened the door, and led her trembling charge into the room, but she no sooner glanced at Everard, than she sighed deeply, and sinking into a chair, covered her face with her hands.

Everard frowned darkly, when he saw that our heroine was accompanied by Mrs. Rayborne; but the agitated state of the poor girl, whose feelings, he was torturing to such an extreme, did appear for a moment to move him, and he stood silently gazing at her for a short time, and seemed hesitating what to say, and half repenting of the unfeeling course he had pursued.

"Mrs. Rayborne," he said at last, in haughty accents, "I need not suggest to you, I presume, that I wish this this interview to be a strictly private one, and you will therefore see the propriety of immediately retiring, especially as Miss Clarence will not stand in any need of your presence."

"Unless it is the wish of my young friend, sir, I shall certainly not comply with your request;" returned Mrs. Rayborne, with equal haughtiness. "I will remain with my young friend, unless she desires me to leave her, for, allow me to say, sir, the hasty and unforbearing temper you have shown throughout the whole of this transaction (at least, as far as I have witnessed it) under the affliction she at present labours, renders it necessary that she should have some sincere friend by her side to advise and support her. You can proceed, sir, but I do not leave this room, unless Miss Ethelinde, as I before said, requests me to do so."

Our heroine looked up through her tears most gratefully towards her kind friend Mrs. Rayborne, who again sought to reassure her by one of her kindest smiles. Everard Welford bit his lips, and traversed the apartment for a second or two hastily, and as if contemplating

within himself how to act. He saw plainly enough that Mrs. Rayborne was determined; that she was not the kind of woman to be easily daunted, and he hesitated as to the course he should pursue, feeling assured that it required the nicest delicacy, the greatest shrewdness to carry his main point into effect, and that one slip of judgment, on his part, might render all his plans abortive.

He began almost to regret that he had urged the interview under the circumstances, especially when he saw the pale countenance and agitated demeanour of the fair object of his persecution, and could he have done so, with any degree of self-dignity, for the reader will not require to be told that he had a superabundant stock of vanity, he would have done so with an apology.

But he considered he had proceeded almost too far to recede, and he therefore resolved, (calling a little more judgment and prudence to his aid) to prosecute his designs to the utmost.

Turning to Mrs. Rayborne with a mock bland smile, he said,—

"I thank you, madam, for reminding me of that, which might otherwise perhaps, have escaped my memory. Your presence will be necessary to bear witness to that I have to state, and in fact it materially concerns you. Your son is the individual who has supplanted me in the affections of Ethelinde Clarence, who has ——"

"Oh, Mr. Welford," sobbed forth our heroine, interrupting him, and sinking on her knees before him, from which degrading position Mrs. Rayborne immediately raised her, "do not proceed. Did I, I demand candidly from you, ever give you any encouragement beyond that of friendship and esteem. Did I by one single act or observation of mine ever give you reason to hope that I could look upon you as my future husband? Oh, no, my conscience acquits me of having done so, for without any disparagement to either your personal or intrinsic qualifications, sir, my choice had fallen upon one whom my heart assured me would never abuse my confidence. It had no room for a second individual, except my amiable parent.

"Norman Rayborne," returned Everard, with a look of the utmost mortification and rage, "I understand you, Ethe.

linde Clarence. It is he that has superseded me in your love.

"I never loved *you*, Everard Welford," resorted the damsel disdainfully, "and therefore why should I hesitate or fear to acknowledge that Norman Rayborne does, and has possessed my heart? The respect which I have hitherto entertained towards you, if *that* was of any value in your eyes, you are taking great pains by your present cruel, and unwarrantable conduct, to deprive yourself of. Am I, I ask you, not the mistress of my own affections?"

"True, Miss Clarence," replied Everard, with a sardonic smile, "I am ready to admit that you are the mistress of your affections; that they may be placed at your will upon any object, let that object be ever so worthy or unworthy.— You are not the mistress of your destiny, neither can you set aside those circumstances, nor cancel that compact, which makes you mine. Nay, frown not contemptuously, for you will find that I am making no empty boast."

"Mr. Welford," interposed Mrs. Rayborne, indignantly, and unable to control the expression of her feelings, especially when she beheld the cool assurance of Everard; "are you a man, are you a gentleman, that you can address such language to a poor girl already so worn down by sorrow and affliction?—Shame on you, shame on you, sir!"

"You may spare yourself the trouble of rebuking me, madam," replied Everard, with a look of contempt, "for I assure you that it has not the slightest effect on me. I come here armed with facts that must and shall carry me out in the objects I have in view, and let any one dare to obstruct them at their peril. I say let Ethelinde Clarence venture to oppose them if she values not her own credit, or the life of her father. I now call upon her, in your presence, Mrs. Rayborne, to retract the vows she has acknowledged to have made to your son, and promise to forget him—forget him entirely, for he must henceforth be a stranger to her—and to pledge herself to become mine."

"Oh, never! never, by Heaven!" solemnly and firmly replied Ethelinde.

"Beware!" cried the impatient and enraged Everard; "you little anticipate what the consequences of your refusal, to yourself and those who are connected with you will be. Again I ask you, will you promise me to abjure the vows you have made to Norman Rayborne?"

"Never!" replied Ethelinde, firmly; "he alone it is who possesses my heart, and if fate so wills it that he shall not become my husband—no other man shall ever receive my hand."

Everard took two or three hasty strides across the apartment, and muttered some incoherent curses to himself, and then turning with an inflamed and infuriated aspect towards our heroine, he exclaimed,—

"Ethelinde Clarence, once more I caution you to be mindful of what you say, and make no rash vows. I once more repeat that, years ago, your father bound himself by a solemn vow that you should not become the bride of any other man than myself, and on the ratification of that vow depends his life!"

A thrill of horror ran through the veins of Ethelinde, as Everard uttered these words, and completely unnerved her. The fearful truth of his assertions was too evident, after what her father had himself acknowledged, for her any longer to doubt them, and she was placed in a dilemma, from which she knew not how to escape. She threw herself with a burst of emotion, which we cannot attempt to describe, upon her knees before him, and with a look which ought to have moved even the most obdurate heart to forbearance, she ejaculated,—

"Oh, Mr. Welford, you cannot be so cruel, so entirely destitute of all feeling as to persist in this unnatural demand. Think you that Heaven will ever sanction the fulfilment of a vow exacted under such circumstances? Or, that even should you triumph in the accomplishment of your wishes, that any real happiness can ever attend your union with one who has again and again candidly assured you that she has no heart to bestow upon you. Reflect, reflect I beseech you, on the cruelty of your persecution (for by no other term, harsh though it may appear to be, can I call it), and I feel satisfied that your natural good sense, and your feelings as a man, will induce you to act with forbear ance. Oh, why seek to dissever the bonds of friendship by which we have hitherto been united? If you sincerely wish my happiness, you will abandon a suit which meets with no response in my bosom, and by the generous forfeiture of your own hopes, make me for ever your debtor and admirer, though I cannot be your lover. I implore you, for my own sake, for the sake of my poor father, not to turn a deaf ear to my supplications. Whatever may have been that parent's faults (and Heaven knows, I never deemed him capable of being guilty of any), I entreat you to bury them in oblivion. Thus will you have performed a part that must ever be most satisfactory to your own conscience and will likewise have a claim on and ensure you my everlasting gratitude."

Any one would suppose that the simple and affecting eloquence of this appeal, and the tone in which it was expressed, could not have failed to have had its due effect upon Everard Welford, and that he would immediately have withdrawn, after having made an apology; but it was not so. On the contrary, he seemed to become the more excited and exasperated, as the extent of our heroine's aversion became the more apparent; and Ethelinde perceiving the utter hopelessness of her supplications, and the inflexibility of the man to whom she appealed, arose from her knees, and throwing herself into Mrs. Rayborne's arms, burst into tears.

"Mr. Welford," said Mrs. Rayborne, "You see the condition of this girl, and you surely cannot think of prolonging this interview?"

"Madam," replied Everard, with his usual haughtiness, "your officious interference, allow me to assure you, will not have the slightest effect upon me; I came here not to be trifled with, nor to have my intentions so easily defeated as you may imagine. I may appear cruel, obstinate, and unreasonable; but that I cannot help, neither do I regard it in the least. My business will neither admit of delay, or the standing upon delicate trifles. I demand from Miss Clarence, a plain and candid answer to a simple question; is she prepared to forget Norman Rayborne, and to receive my addresses?"

"No, no, by Heaven, never!" fervently and solemnly replied Ethelinde.

Everard Welford bit his lips, and his whole frame was convulsed with the most ungovernable rage.

"Very well," he said, in a hoarse voice, which conveyed a fearful meaning; "then Ethelinde Clarence holds the honour, the life of her father, in no estimation!"

"Oh, base calumny!" exclaimed the deeply-agitated Ethelinde; "what sacrifice is there that I would not make, to save a life so precious to me?"

"I have put you to the test," said Everard; "on your word, your promise, your father's life depends."

"Hideous assertion," cried Ethelinde; "it cannot be true—I will not, I cannot believe it!"

"Of what use is this obstinacy?" said Everard. "I hold the proofs, the incontestible proofs of your father's guilt, (since you will compel me to speak in the presence of a witness), in my power. Consent to become mine, and they shall for ever more be buried in oblivion."

"Spare me, Everard, I implore you!"

"Nay, I must have a candid, and unequivocal answer."

"I cannot promise that from which my heart revolts with an indescribable feeling of horror."

"Then be the consequences on your own head," answered Everard; "since you thus scornfully reject and insult me, you cannot be surprised that I should be provoked to do the worst in my power."

"Mr. Welford," ejaculated Mrs. Rayborne, unable to restrain her indignant feelings, "this language unmans you, and—"

"Madam," interrupted Everard, scornfully, "I care nothing whatever for your opinion; and allow me to repeat that your interference is uncalled for, and will be of no avail. Ethelinde has set me at defiance, and I will therefore speak out, and let the world know of what crime her father has been guilty, and by which he has forfeited his life to the offended laws of his country. Myself and my father hold the proofs in our hands, by which his certain conviction would be inevitable."

"Oh, horror! horror!" groaned Ethelinde;—"but 'tis false, false as he whose polluted lips dare to give utterance to it."

"Will you still persist, obstinate girl," said Everard, "in braving me to the disclosure?"

"I will," firmly replied our heroine; "nothing can possibly be more torturing than this terrible suspense. Give vent to your foul calumny at once, Everard Welford, even though the revelation strike me dead; such is the state of desperation to which you have aroused me, that I am prepared to hear it."

"Once more I warn you to reflect ere you demand the frightful disclosure, which it is in your power to silence for ever;" said Everard.

"Forbear, forbear, young man," exclaimed Mrs. Rayborne; "this conduct is monstrous. Ethelinde, my love, you shall no longer remain here, to have your ears insulted, and your feelings wounded. Come, come, my poor girl, let us retire, and probably when Mr. Welford is left to himself, he will deeply repent as he ought to do, that he should so grossly have committed himself."

"Nay," said Everard, determinedly, and placing his back against the door; "Ethelinde Clarence shall not quit this room, until I have fully spoken my my mind. I am not a man to be trifled with, and that both you and her should have discovered ere this time. Let her grant the promise I have endeavoured to extract from her, and not only shall the lips of me and my father, be for ever sealed upon the subject, but the proofs, the fatal, the indubitable proofs of her father's guilt, shall be immediately destroyed. Once more, I ask you, Ethelinde, will you consent to my wishes?"

"Oh, Everard," said the distracted girl, weeping bitterly; "once more, I appeal to your mercy. Do not, I implore you, urge me to that which is so repugnant to my feelings, and my hopes."

"This is trifling," said Everard, impatiently. "I require an explicit answer. Will you or not, promise me to receive my addresses?"

"I cannot," replied our heroine.

"You will not," said Everard.

"I will not," returned Ethelinde, positively.

"Enough," said Everard Welford, with a bitter scowl; "then I am to understand that you brave the consequences which are involved in such a preremptory refusal?"

"Surely, sir, common courtesy, gallantry, and proper feeling towards our sex, ought to induce you to act with more forbearance," said Mrs. Rayborne; "and at any rate, under the melancholy circumstances in which my young friend, Miss Clarence, is at present placed, to allow her some time for reflection upon the peculiarly delicate subject which you propose. Heaven knows, that her mind must at present be sufficiently distracted, without its being further disturbed by the threats and insinuations you have thrown out, and allow me to say——"

"You have said enough madam," hastily interrupted Everard; "and I certainly know not which to admire the most, your impertinence or presumption, in addressing me in the way you have done."

"I have merely appealed to you, sir," retorted Mrs. Rayborne, with the most cutting sarcasm; "as a man, I have merely appealed to your humanity, your feelings as a gentleman, and the common reason with which we have an undoubted right to expect all our fellow-creatures endowed, especially a person of the pretentions of Mr. Everard Welford; but, finding that you are entirely destitute of either quality, I shall not trouble myself, I shall not *condesend* to hold any further argument with you."

Again Everard Welford bit his lips, and he could not help writhing under the just and severe rebuke which was conveyed to him in the pointed observations of Mrs. Rayborne. He fixed upon her a look of indignation which she met with one of utter contempt, and then strode several times across the room in a state of the most violent agitation.

"Confusion!" he muttered to himself, but still sufficiently loud to reach the ears of Mrs. Rayborne, and the trembling Ethelinde; "am I to be insulted, braved, when I hold everything in my power, and one word of mine could bring them to destruction."

"Oh, Mr. Welford," once more supplicated our heroine, clasping her hands together, and fixing upon him a look which might have moved the most insensible heart; "forbear, forbear; you will surely after this repent having acted in the manner you have done, towards a now almost unprotected female. Give me, I beg of you, time to reflect upon what you have said, and then if reason does not tell you to yield to my decision, I must endeavour to submit to whatever your feelings or vindictive passions may tempt you to do."

"Ethelinde Clarence," said Everard, in a rude and determined tone, "I have suffered myself to be trifled with by your fooling, but I am resolved no longer to give way to such weakness. It needs but one word for you to decide me in the course I shall pursue. Will you receive me as your accepted suitor?"

"That question I have already answered;" returned Ethelinde in a faint voice, but still assuming all the firmness she could.

"Then you seal your father's doom!"

"Oh, no, no, no!—You have it not in your power to injure him."

"I can substantiate against him a charge that will bring him to the gallows!" replied Everard, in a tone of voice which froze the very blood in the veins of Ethelinde and Mrs. Rayborne.

"'Tis false!" exclaimed the former, for a moment mustering courage. "Of what crime dare you accuse him?"

"You dare me to make the statement?"

"I do," returned Ethelinde, "because my heart convinces me that it is a base fabrication; a cold-blooded asertion upon the character of one who could never have offered the slightest injury towards any of his fellow creatures."

"Then you still doubt the truth of what I say?"

"I do," replied Ethelinde, worked up to a pitch of desperation; "of what crime dare you accuse my dear, my amiable father?"

"Will you persist in bearding me to an answer?" said Everard. "Are you determined that I should give utterance to that which will bring eternal shame upon your name?"

"Yes, yes," said our heroine, "you have taken the most unmanly advantage of my present unprotected state, Mr. Welford, to throw out insinuations of the most vile description. I do not, I cannot believe them, and at all hazards, I demand an explanation. Again I demand, of what crime dare you accuse my unfortunate father?"

"Of a crime," replied Everard, "of which my father and I hold the incon-testible proofs. Of a crime which was committed against my parent, and for which but, for his forbearance, yourfather, Ethelinde Clarence, would, years ago, have been consigned to the hands of the hangman."

"Horror! horror!" shrieked the appalled Ethelinde, and fixing upon the heartless Everard a look which was sufficient to sink him into shame! but he remained completely unmoved, so entirely had he made up his mind to have a positive answer to his proposition on that very day. "It is an atrocious falsehood; it cannot be, it is totally impossible!"

"You dare me to the proof, Ethelinde Clarence," observed Everard. "Beware, and do not force me to a revelation which it is in your power to withhold, and by one single word to bury it for ever, as I have before told you, in oblivion."

"Mr. Welford," interceded Mrs. Rayborne, in mild and persuasive accents, "seeing the state in which my amiable young friend is, surely you cannot be so destitute of all feeling as to proceed to such extremities as those which you have threatened."

"Madam," replied Everard, with the most inexorable haughtiness and determination; "I have nothing more to observe to you, than to repeat that enough has been said on that subject, and that my mind is fully made up, let the consequences be what they may. I have been scorned, insulted, and defied. The truth of what I have asserted has been impugned, and it is my place, in justice to myself, to shew that I do not make statements which I cannot fully substantiate. It is, as I have before observed, still in the power of Ethelinde to silence my tongue on the painful subject for ever; this interview has already been protracted too long, and I therefore now once more ask you, Ethelinde Clarence, whether you will consent to to receive the addresses which I offer you with all sincerity and ardour, with favour, and to think no more of Norman Rayborne?"

"By Heaven!" exclaimed the poor girl, "to whose mercy and protection I appeal, I will never make a vow so utterly contrary to all my feelings, my hopes, my wishes."

"Then hear me, proud and obstinate girl," returned Everard Welford, his countenance at the same time inflamed with rage, "in a short time, should your wretched father recover from his present illness, he will assuredly be denounced to the world as the perpetrator of——"

"Of what?" demanded Ethelinde and Mrs. Rayborne, in a breath.

"Of the crime of FORGERY!" replied Everard, in a hollow voice.

Ethelinde uttered one appalling shriek, that might have struck awe into even the stoutest breast, and immediately

EHTELINDE WATCHING BY THE COUCH OF HER SICK FATHER.

swooned in the arms of her scarcely less astonished and terrified friend.

A fearful pause of some moments ensued, during which time Everard gazed at his pale and inanimate victim with mingled feelings of exultation, revenge, and regret. It was impossible that he could help feeling some degree of shame at the brutal (for no other term can we reasonably apply to it) part he had acted, and he almost wished that he had not proceeded so far; but it was now too late to retrace his steps, and whatever might be the result, he was determined—fully determined to proceed with his plot.

Mrs. Rayborne, as she supported the insensible form of our unfortunate heroine in her arms, fixed upon Everard a look of the utmost disgust, and reproach, and after a pause, during which she was endeavouring to control her indignant feelings, she ejaculated—

"Oh, Everard Welford, could I ever have believed that you could have been guilty of such inhuman conduct as this? Can a man who has evinced such malicious, such vindictive feelings presume to aspire to the love—to the hand of one so lovely, so gentle, and so virtuous? You have disgraced yourself, sir, eternally disgraced yourself, and should be ashamed again to obtrude your presence upon this poor, afflicted, and innocent girl, who it is impossible can ever henceforth view you with any other feelings than those of the most thorough alarm and abhorrance."

"Indeed, madam," said Everard with a frown; "that is your opinion it seems, for which, allow me to assure you I entertain the most superlative contempt. Norman Rayborne may be beloved by Ethelinde Clarence, but he shall never possess her hand; mark my words, never!—I have spoken the truth, I have been provoked to it, and am ready to abide by the consequences."

"And can you gaze upon the pale countenance of this poor girl, can you recollect the situation of her father, unmoved, and without experiencing the least sensation of regret and self-reproach, at the conduct you have pursued?" demanded Mrs. Rayborne, in an impressive manner, at the same time fixing her penetrating eyes upon the countenance of him she addressed.

"I have nothing more to say to you, Mrs. Rayborne," answered Everard, "than merely to suggest to you that if you are really the friend to Miss Ethelinde Clarence that you profess to be, you will advise her to reflect well upon what I have said, and not to aggravate me to proceed to extremities, which I would fain avoid. It is still in her power to prevent such results as those which will most certainly follow, should she continue obstinate; and if she really loves her father she will not hesitate a

moment. I wish you good morning, Mrs. Rayborne."

With these words Everard Welford haughtily stalked from the room, before Mrs. Rayborne had time to make any reply. The feelings which occupied the bosom of the amiable woman at that moment, we need not attempt to describe; but her whole attention was now directed to our heroine, and she resolved to see immediately towards her recovery. She rang the bell, and Jane promptly attended the summons. Ethelinde was quickly conveyed to her chamber, and Doctor Charlton was also apprised of her situation, and hastened to render his assistance, Mr. Clarence being so far composed that he could be left.

CHAPTER V.

MORE TROUBLES FOR ETHELINDE.—THE SECRET.—THE FATAL VOW.

WE will pass over several days subsequent to the facts recorded in the last chapter, as nothing of sufficient importance occurred to be worthy of any particular notice. Everard Welford had been called suddenly away to a distant part of the country on business; which was a source of no inconsiderable relief to Ethelinde, who could not even think upon his name without feelings of the greatest terror.

A favourable change had taken place in Mr. Clarence, and the worthy doctor pronounced it as his opinion that he would be restored to convalescence.

With what painful anxiety did poor Ethelinde watch by the side of his couch, and with what feelings of horror did she reflect upon the terrible words of Everard Welford, and daily, hourly, expected, and dreaded a confirmation from her father's lips. She almost feared to meet the gaze of that revered parent, lest he should read the thoughts which were passing in her mind, and in consequence of the excitement which it would naturally be the cause of, he should suffer a relapse, which in his present delicate state would in all probability prove fatal.

But it could not be true; the accusation of Everard Welford must be a base, an atrocious calumny. Could she look in the benevolent countenance of her father, and remember all his numerous noble, virtuous, and generous acts, and believe him to have been guilty of the crime which Everard had stated? It was impossible. And yet had he not himself declared to her his guilt, and how could she reasonably any longer entertain a doubt?—The idea was dreadful, and it was not without the greatest difficulty, the most severe trial of her feelings, that she could conceal the thoughts which so heavily oppressed her, from that beloved being who was the subject of her agony and anxiety.

The recent conduct of Everard Welford convinced her that he was at heart a villain, and she could not think of him with any other sentiments than those of disgust, fear, and abhorrence. To be placed at the mercy of such a man was dreadful in the extreme, but to view him in the character of her future husband, was an idea almost too revolting for her reason to endure. It could never be; that Almighty Being, who ever watches over innocence would surely never permit so cruel a sacrifice. Something, she endeavoured to hope, would yet transpire to release her and her father from his power, and to enable them to set his threats at defiance. Her vows were solemnly plighted to Norman Rayborne, and though they might never meet again, she felt convinced that no other man could ever supplant him in her heart's warmest affections.

Oh, what a striking contrast did the character of him she loved, and Everard Welford present. And what would be his indignation, his sufferings, did he know the painful position in which she was placed, and was aware of the brutal conduct of his rival towards her. But she thanked Providence that he was in ignorance of it, for she wished not to add to the torture which a separation from her must have caused him.

When she was alone, she recalled to her memory all the words he had uttered on the melancholy night of their parting, and many were the tears she shed, as they rushed upon her brain.

"Alas!" she sighed, "and shall I be compelled to break the solemn vow I made to you, dear Norman, at parting?

Oh, forbid it Heaven, and interpose to save me from a fate which is by far too horrible for contemplation."

And yet what cause had she to entertain the least hope. The threats of Everard Welford were quite sufficient to convince her that he was determined, and as to expecting any forbearance from a man of his character, it would have been preposterous to have entertained such an idea for a moment. Certainly nothing could be more wretched than than the prospect which was spread before her, and she shrunk appalled from the bare contemplation of it. But it was necessary that she should struggle with her feelings, or she would never be able to support the trials to which she was sure to be subjected.

Mrs. Rayborne and her daughter daily visited her, and by their kind and earnest exertions, they did succeed in somewhat composing her feelings, and in leading her to hope that something would yet occur to release her from the persecution of Everard Welford, whom they could not, after what had taken place, but thoroughly abhor and despise, and they congratulated Ethelinde on his absence from home, and sincerely hoped that something would occur to detain him until she had quite recovered from the shock occasioned by his last interview.

But Ethelinde was not sanguine upon this point; she felt satisfied that he would not delay his return a moment longer than was unavoidable, and that he would then immediately renew his hateful importunities, from which she shrunk with feelings almost amounting to horror. It was also impossible that she could much longer conceal from her father what had taken place, and she felt severely for the anguish and remorse he would be sure to experience, when he was made acquainted with it.

Mr. Clarence at length so far recovered that he was able to leave his chamber, and, supported on the arm of his lovely daughter, to take an airing in the extensive gardens attached to the mansion, and while Ethelinde felt the most unbounded gratitude to Providence for his recovery, she still contemplated with horror the divulgement of that fearful secret which reason too well assured her, both from what had transpired from Everard Welford and her father himself, would involve so critical, if not fatal a crisis in both their destinies. Oh, how anxiously did she hope that Providence would avert the evils which evidently impended over them, not for her own sake, for life under all the trying circumstances, which had recently taken place, had become valueless to her, but for that of her beloved parent, whose grey hairs she wished to see descend to the grave untarnished with shame, and with the same respect and veneration in which he was now universally held.

As the poor old man leaned upon her arm, and looked affectionately in her countenance, he sighed deeply, and it was quite evident that his mind was suffering a tempest of the most torturing feeling. Had he but known what his lovely daughter had had to endure during the last few days from the persecution of Everard Welford, had he been aware of the brutal assertions, the unmanly feelings that young man had made and displayed, how doubly keen would have been his sufferings.

"You are pale, child, haggard," he suddenly observed, as they paused in their walk and seated themselves beneath the umbrageous foliage of a noble chesnut tree. "You are not the same rosy, laughing Ethelinde that you were some few months since."

"My dear father," sighed our heroine, "can you expect me to be so, after the agonizing care and anxiety to which I have recently been subjected by your alarming accident, and when I was hourly in fear of losing my best friend, my parent, my only natural protector. But—but, I will endeavour to be happy now, dear father; the Almighty has been good and merciful in restoring you to me, and henceforth I will endeavour to resume that cheerful aspect which has hitherto afforded you so much satisfaction and delight."

How beautiful did Ethelinde Clarence appear as she uttered these words, and yet how terrible were the feelings which were passing in her mind at that moment.

Her father seized her hand, and while he fixed upon her a look which shewed at once the intensity of his own agony, he replied, in a voice half choked with the conflicting power of his emotions,—

"No, no, my darling Ethelinde, in your affection you would deceive me as to the real state of your feelings, but it cannot be."

"Deceive you, father?"

"Yes, child, yes; but from a most virtuous motive. Oh, God! that it should ever come to this!"

"Father, dearest father," ejaculated Ethelinde, "what mean you? For the love of Heaven, explain yourself, and do not—oh! do not keep me in this terrible state of suspense."

"You love Norman Rayborne, Ethelinde?"

She averted her blushing countenance and replied not, but it needed no deep penetration to discover the answer she would have returned if she had had the power to do so.

"You cannot regard Everard Welford," continued her father, "as your future husband?"

"Oh, never, never!" replied our heroine, energetically; "his very name inspires me with terror. Father, beloved father, I am prepared to die, but never, never can I, will I, become the bride of Everard Welford; and yet——"

"And yet what, Ethelinde?"

"Oh, I dare not utter it. Alas! what an unfeeling being must he have been to have given utterance to the words!"

"Ah!" exclaimed Mr. Clarence, eagerly, and at the same time trembling in every limb with the apprehensions which so fast crowded upon his imagination. "You have seen him then? Tell me, tell me, quick."

"I—I have."

"Ah, my conscience told me that something had occurred to distract your mind, my poor child, even more than that anxiety which you felt in consequence of the accident which had befallen me. Oh! would to Heaven that that accident had proved fatal!"

"Oh, my father, forbear; say not so," observed the agitated Ethelinde.

"Ethelinde," demanded Mr. Clarence, "do you then mean to say that Everard Welford has advanced his addresses to you during my illness?"

"He has, father."

"And held out threats?"

"Alas! alas!"

"Miscreant!"

"But it is not true, my parent?—say it is not; it is too horrible to be believed."

"Ah!" cried Mr. Clarence, in a state of the most indescribable agitation; "did he, then, proceed so far? Oh, coward, villain! and you, my poor child, to suffer treatment such as this."

"Do not give way to this emotion, my dear father, I beg of you," said Ethelinde; "but endeavour ——"

"Ethelinde, Ethelinde!" interrupted her father, while his bosom heaved with the most convulsive emotions; "you should look upon me with disgust, horror, contempt, hatred!"

"Oh, dreadful!" gasped forth our heroine, and she stared aghast into the pallid countenance of her distracted parent. "You mean not what you say. Some terrible imagination—the result of your recent unfortunate accident, has temporarily taken possession of your reason."

"No, no, girl," said Mr. Clarence, impatiently, "it is not so. My reason is, alas! too keen; would that it had fled for ever, or that it had pleased the Almighty to take me to himself. Yes, Ethelinde, you behold before you, in the character of your parent, a poor, guilty, miserable wretch! One who has disgraced himself, and thrown a blight—a withering blight—upon all your youthful and virtuous hopes. My liberty, my life, is in the hands of Everard Welford and his father. To save them, I have sacrificed you. I have made a vow that you shall become the wife of Everard; and either you must yield, or I submit to a horrible, an ignominious fate."

"Great God!" exclaimed Ethelinde; "then what Everard asserted appears to be too fatally true."

"Of what did he accuse me, Ethelinde?" with breathless haste, demanded Major Clarence, and his whole frame was so violently agitated, that had it not been for the support of his daughter, he must have sunk to the ground.

"Oh! urge me not, father," she replied; "some other time, when both of us may be better prepared to listen to these painful, these dreadful explanations. Would to Heaven that there was no necessity for them, that the fearful subject of them could be buried in oblivion altogether."

"Nay, Ethelinde," ejaculated Mr. Clarence, "it will admit no delay; there is that upon my mind which must be divulged, and though I should die in the effort to disclose it, I am determined to do so. Of what did Everard Welford accuse me?"

"Spare me, father!"

"Speak! speak!"

"Oh, he surely could not truly accuse you of anything that you should feel ashamed or afraid yourself to acknowledge."

"He can!" replied Mr. Clarence, with an agonizing groan; oh, I acknowledge myself to have been most guilty."

"No, no, father, dear father, recall those words;" said the deeply afflicted Ethelinde.

"I cannot, my poor child," he replied, in the most melancholy accents, "for they are the truth. Oh, my child, the confidence you place in my integrity wounds me more than all. As you now look upon me, methinks I can see the countenance of your sainted, your patient, your devoted, your gentle mother, as she gazed upon me in sorrow, in heart-rending sorrow, not reproach, when the certainty of my guilt was made but too apparent to her. Oh, Ethelinde, what a wretch have I been. My imprudence, my mad extravagance plunged me into ruin and disgrace, and the knowledge of that was the means of consigning one of the best of women, of wives, and of parents to a premature grave. It was then that the full punishment of my offences came upon me, I was caught in the meshes of those who had long been waiting to entrap me; and what did I then, coward, wretch that I was? To save myself from ignominious punishment, I made that fatal vow, which bartered away the future happiness of my only offspring, and has left you no other alternative, my deeply injured girl, than to become the bride of Everard Welford, or to have me, your father, denounced to the world as a felon!"

"Oh, God! oh, God!" groaned the horror-struck Ethelinde, grasping her father's arm convulsively, and looking into his countenance, as if she would penetrate his very soul; "say not so, my honoured parent, you to whom every person looks up with reverence; you must be labouring under some frightful delusion, the effects of your late alarming accident."

"No, no, my child," returned her father, "it is no delusion, would to Heaven that it was. I repeat, that you ought to shudder to look upon me, since by my crimes I have condemned you to that which must ultimately break your heart; I have doomed you to one who has proved himself to be so heartless a villain; to become the wife of Everard Welford."

"Oh, recall those words, my father," ejaculated our heroine; "they strike horror to my soul; I cannot, I will not ever become the wife of one whom I cannot but loathe and despise."

"Ethelinde," answered Mr. Clarence, solemnly, and with an expression of agony and despair, which no language can properly describe; "then better would it have been had your wretched father's remains ere now been consigned to the tomb."

"Oh, Heaven teach me how to act," cried Ethelinde, beating her breast; "surely I must be labouring under the effects of some frightful dream; there cannot be any real foundation for the dreadful accusation which Everard Welford lately brought against you. Oh, no! I know my beloved, my estimable parent too well, for a moment to entertain such a foul aspersion upon his character."

"You torture me, Ethelinde, by the expression of a confidence which I so little merit. Oh, how unworthy am I to be the parent of so amiable, so innocent a child!"

"Oh! my father, do not, I beseech you, thus unworthily reproach yourself. What conduct of mine can ever adequately repay the kindness, the indulgence, the attention, the care, and affection I have experienced from you? But I dare not, I cannot bring my mind to believe that you are so much in the power of Everard and his father, as you have represented yourself to be."

"Ethelinde, I repeat that I am entirely at their mercy. My life is in their hands and your's."

"Heaven help me, then," groaned the distracted Ethelinde, clasping her hands; "for I am doomed to perpetual misery!"

"Alas! alas!" sighed the wretched Mr. Clarence, striking his forehead; "it is I, guilty man that I am, who have doomed you to misery and despair. But no, it shall not be. It is I who alone have been guilty, and it is I who only should and will fall the sacrifice. Ethelinde, I once more demand of you, and do not hesitate to reply, of what did Everard Welford accuse me?"

"Oh! I must not, dare not name it," returned Ethelinde; "the words would choke me. But after all, I cannot believe otherwise than that it is a cruel fabrication."

"Ethelinde," ejaculated her father, his patience completely exhausted; "I insist upon knowing. The time for explanation has arrived—perhaps it had better not have been deferred so long—and notwithstanding the consequences which may ensue, I will not shrink from it."

"Another time, I implore you, my dear sire. You have not yet sufficient strength to support such a trial of your feelings."

"I am prepared for everthing, my child. I shall never be in a more fit condition for the explanation, and therefore it had better take place now."

Still did Ethelinde hesitate, and knew not how to comply with that which her father demanded of her. To repeat the words of Everard was dreadful, and yet she saw no possibility of doing so. And what added to her despair and anguish was the acknowledgment which her father had made of his guilt, and in that confession she saw at once that she was placed upon the verge of a precipice, from which nothing whatever could extricate her. It was a severe trial for the poor girl, and it was a wonder that her heart did not break under it.

"Will you then, indeed, still urge me, father?" she said, at length. "Will you compel me to a disclosure from which my heart revolts?"

"It must be spoken," replied Mr. Clarence; "and therefore why should it longer be delayed? Courage, my poor girl, and tell me everything that passed between you and Everard Welford, at your short interview with each other. You will find that I will listen with patience and fortitude, however trying it may, as I am sure it will, be to my feelings."

It was indeed a terrible task for our heroine to accomplish, and it was wonderful how she was enabled to do so; but at length the whole fearful truth was divulged.

Mr. Clarence had listened to her in solemn silence, although the heaving of his chest plainly shewed the deep mental anguish he was undergoing all the time; and when she had concluded, he beat his breast, averted his looks, covered his face with his hands, and sobbed aloud.

Etheline flew to him, and throwing her fair arms around his neck, called tenderly upon his name, and begged of him to look up, and and remove the dreadful weight which pressed upon her heart, by assuring her of his innocence.

Mr. Clarence did, indeed, after a brief interval, raise his eyes towards his daughter, but their expression was that of horror and despair, and Ethelinde was quite awe-struck at the remarkable and ghastly change which had come over him in so short a space of time. He fixed his earnest gaze upon her, but for some time was totally incapable of speaking. The agitation, the agonising suspense of Ethelinde during this interval may be easily imagined. She saw too much from her unfortunate father's demeanour to give her any reason to expect anything else but the confirmation of her most terrible apprehensions.

"Oh, God, my sweet, my dutiful, my affectionate child," at length ejaculated Mr. Clarence, "how do I shrink and tremble in your presence, as the dreadful recollection of the past rushes with overwelming force upon my memory. I repeat, Ethelinde, that you should hate, you should despise me, you should turn from me with a shudder of horror and disgust. I am a wretch, unworthy of your love; would to Heaven I had never survived this recent accident."

"Oh, terrible, my father!" exclaimed our heroine with a look of unbounded terror; "do not, for the sake of the love you bear me, give utterance to such dreadful words; your mind has not yet recovered from the severe shock you have lately received. Everard Welford must have basely, maliciously, and cruelly misrepresented the facts."

"Alas! alas!" groaned Major Clarence, "he has too fearfully spoken the truth. I am all, nay more than he has represented me to be. I have sacrificed you, Ethelinde, I have sold you to one whom I now discover to be a heartless scoundrel; my crimes, my folly, if I may call it by so mild a term, broke your poor mother's heart. Oh, I have been most guilty; Heaven pardon me, for I feel most keenly the weight of my offences."

The poor old man once more covered his face with his hands, and sobbed as if his heart would break. Ethelinde threw her arms again around her father's neck, she pressed affectionate kisses upon his venerable cheeks, and endeavoured by all those gentle and eloquent, but silent persuasions, of which her lively sex alone can speak the language in its true essence, to soothe him into composure.

"Father, dear father," she at length found strength sufficient to articulate, "let us retire into the house, and there seek to compose your feelings. Your mind is harrassed by torturing feelings, which I cannot consider to be correct or just. You are condemning yourself for that of which I cannot, I will not believe you guilty. We will waive this painful subject for the present, for we are neither of us in a condition to enter upon it. Come, come, dear father, let us return, and to-morrow, if you feel better, we will enter into the explanation in which the happiness of us both is so deeply involved."

"Your feelings have been outraged, girl," said Mr. Clarence, his bosom swelling with indignation; "you have been subjected to insult, I am convinced of it, and I have been the primary, the only cause of all."

"Oh, no, no, no, not so, dear father," said the affectionate Ethelinde, clasping his hand and endeavouring to lead him from the spot.

"I have, I have," answered Mr. Clarence, "I dare not attempt to deny it. Oh, what a fearful blight has my misconduct, my poor girl, thrown upon all your youthful prospects. Ethelinde, I am a wretch, and unworthy of your love."

"Forbear, forbear, for Heaven's sake, unless you would drive me mad. What can my revered parent ever have done that I should cease to pay him the homage and heart-felt love of a daughter."

All, everything, and more than Everard Welford has stated," replied Mr. Clarence, with a shudder of horror. "Ethelinde it fills me with tenfold shame and remorse to witness the looks of unmerited tenderness and compassion which you fix upon me. Would to God that I were in the silent tomb."

"Oh, Heaven forbid," fervently exclaimed the deeply agonized Ethelinde, "what would become of me, especially under the present existing and alarming circumstances, were I deprived of your protection."

"My protection, poor persecuted girl, what a bitter mockery is it to apply such a term to it. I have no power to defend you from the machinations of those who importune you; on the contrary. I am entirely at your mercy or theirs. The offence I committed in the first instance, was against Mr. Welford; he could have placed me on my trial, and on conviction my life would undoubtedly at that period have been forfeited. Yes, Ethelinde, well may you shudder with horror, but I once more repeat that your father's life would have been sacrificed on the public gallows, had it not been for a compromise with Everard's father!"

"Appalling statement!" cried the terror-stricken Ethelinde, "it is impossible that it can be true!"

"Why do you still doubt the authenticity of my assertions, my unfortunate child? Think you that it is at all likely I would thus accuse myself, if it were not founded in truth? Alas! alas! would that it were not. From that fatal moment I became a slave—a slave to the will, the mercy, and dictation of Everard's father. He knew that if I lived, my future fortunes must be splendid, more than equal to his own, immeasurably more; he took avantage of the power he held over me, and granted me the life I had forfeited, only on condition of my entering into a compact that should you and his son live to the years of maturity, you should become his wife. That compact I entered into—that fatal vow I made—the evidences of my guilt they hold in their hands; they can at any time be brought forward to my convic-

tion, and thus it is, my poor injured child, that you are to become the bride of a man who is hateful to you, and who I am now perfectly satisfied is totally unworthy of your numerous and transcendent virtues, or to see your wretched father consigned to an ignominious fate."

With what indescribable feelings of horror, astonishment, and breathless attention did Ethelinde listen to the fearful statement of her unfortunate father; she saw at once that her doom was sealed—that she was indeed sacrificed to that man whom she could not but fear and detest, after the recent unnatural display he had made, the total disregard he had paid to her feelings, or the fearful situation in which she was placed, and the common respect due to her sex; despair settled upon her heart, and it was not without the greatest difficulty that she could save herself from sinking to the ground.

Major Clarence watched the countenance of his beauteous daughter with a despairing heart, and who shall attempt to describe the intense, the severe anguish and remorse he felt at the same time; all the weight of his past transgressions came with tenfold force upon him; he could not but accuse himself of being the absolute murderer of his offspring, and again and again he wished that she had never been born, or that he had expired before he could have committed the offence which had brought so dreadful a punishment upon him, and plunged the innocent girl whom he so fondly loved, into a vortex of misery and ruin, from which it seemed that nothing could extricate her.

A fearful pause of some seconds ensued, during which time the father and daughter once more sank on the seat they had previously occupied, and remained totally absorbed in their agonizing thoughts, without venturing to look at each other.

Fain would Ethelinde have believed it all a frightful dream; but after what had taken place, it was impossible to do so; the stern reality was too startling, was too apparent to be thus rejected, and the fate in store for her was revealed to her as clearly and distinctly as if reflected in a mirror.

But still she made another effort to

overcome her feelings, and to tranquillize the excited mind of her unfortunate parent, and this time her endeavours were not wholly without success. Fearful and degrading as the partial disclosure which Mr. Claoence had made to his daughter had been to him, still it afforded some slight relief to his mind, and he determined t reveal everything anew, but at present he felt inadequate to the task.

"Dear father," at length said Ethelinde, "Heaven surely will extend its mercy towards us under our present

DOCTOR CHARLTON ENTREATS ETHELINDE TO RETIRE TO REST.

severe trials, and something will occur to avert the dreadful evils which we apprehend. I will endeavour to hope. Come, come, once more I say let us retire into the house, you are yet too weak to undergo such excitement, and we will say no more upon the subject at present. God is good and merciful, and will not inflict upon us more than we have strength to bear."

"My sweet girl, my gentle Ethelinde, said Mr. Clarence, pressing her to his throbbing bosom; "how little do I deserve this; your words instead of being those of hope and consolation, should be those of the bitterest reproach for, but for my crimes, your virtues might have been rewarded by your being made, as you deserve to be, the happiest of the happy."

"And so I shall be, so we both shall be yet, my beloved parent," said the lovely girl, endeavouring to smile through her tears; "notwithstanding all that has taken place, I do not, I will not give way to despair. I am confident that you must be labouring under some fatal error, and that Providence will not suffer our enemies (for as such I must in future regard Mr. Welford and his son) to triumph in their guilty scheme. Come, my father, you require rest and composure after this exciting conversation. You are yet too weak to have your mind harrassed by such subjects."

Major Clarence shook his head mournfully, and sighed deeply.

"Alas! he ejaculated, "what can ever erase the subject from my mind, where it is written in characters of fire? Ah, too lenient an eye. I feel my utter unworthiness, and—"

"Hold! hold!" interrupted our heroine, "I must not, I canot listen to such language as this. My heart assures me that it is unmerited, and that ere long it will be shown how unjustly you reproach yourself. But let us no longer tarry here; I see that your strength is failing you, and therefore let us at once return to the house, lest you should suffer a relapse, which might be productive of consequences I tremble to think upon."

Mr. Clarence suffered his daughter to take his arm, without answering, and to lead him from the spot. They re-entered the house, where he felt so much overpowered by his emotions that he was immediately compelled to seek his couch, and it was not until after our heroine saw him drop gradually off into a calm repose that she ventured to leave his chamber.

CHAPTER VI.

THE RECITAL.

But when Ethelinde was alone in her own apartment, she gave the most uninterrupted indulgence to all the torturing and alarming feelings which distracted her bosom, and pictured to herself, in the most vivid characters, the future horrors that were in store for her.

How could she venture to encourage hope, after the painful observations, the dreadful acknowledgements which her father had made? She would fain have attributed it to a weakness of reason, consequent upon his recent illness, but all that he had said, and so solemnly asserted, was so confirmatory of the statement of Everard Welford, that she could not do so.

He had again and again asserted that he had been guilty of a crime which had placed him at the mercy of the Welfords, and that it was only by her consenting to become the wife of Everard, that he could be rescued from an ignominious fate! Could anything be more terrible than this idea. Our heroine beat her breast in despair, and her tears flowed fast, as she continued to reflect, and the longer she did so, the more cheerless, the more utterly hopeless her prospects seemed to be. To be sacrificed to such a man as Everard Welford, a man entirely destitute of every proper feeling, was so revolting that death would have been preferable, even though it were attended with the most excruciating tortures; but what other alternative was left her, if all that her father had asserted (and which she had no reason to doubt), was correct?

Most bitterly did the poor girl bemoan her fate, and appealed to Omnipotence to know what she had done to merit such a severe punishment.

And must she then give up all thoughts of the generous, the noble-minded Norman Rayborne. Must she be compelled to relinquish all her hopes, to break the solemn vows she had plighted to him, and to leave him to misery and despair? Oh, no, it could not be; reason and every natural feeling revolted from even the contemplation of such a course She determined to make her father acquainted with what had passed between them at their farewell meeting, and to ascertain whether there was no hope of prevailing upon Everard to act with forbearance, and at least for some time to delay the execution of his purpose, for in the meanwhile something might occur by which her father and her would be released from his trammels. However, she had seen too much of the character of Everard, especially lately, to give way to any particularly sanguine hopes upon the subject, and consequently her mind felt but little relief from the cares and anxieties which oppressed it.

Her thoughts followed Norman in his distant journey, and various were the apprehensions she entertained for his safety, and many were the ardent prayers she offered up to Heaven for his protection. He was now exposed to all the perils of the deep, and should angry storms arise, he might probably never reach the place of his destination, but find an ocean grave, far far, away from those who loved him, and whose happiness entirely depended upon his future prosperity.

What agony did that thought impart to her, and for some time her mind was completely abstracted from every other subject. She deeply regretted the hard fate which had compelled Norman to quit his native country; and yet had he remained near her, what encouragement under present circumstances, could she give to his hopes? Alas! she reflected it would most undoubtedly have been much better for them both had they never known each other, since it seemed evident that Providence had so willed it that they should not come together, and therefore what misery would have been saved them. To forget him, Ethelinde felt to be utterly impossible. Oh, no his image was too deeply fixed in the inmost recess of her heart for anything to remove it, and under all circumstances that heart must continue to love him, to worship him, until it should cease to beat.

As these thoughts occurred to her mind, Ethelinde took forth the treasured locket from her bosom, and having pressed it again and again to her lips, wept tears of anguish upon it.

While our heroine was thus engaged, Mrs. Rayborne and her daughter were announced. Their arrival at such a time was most welcome to her, for she much needed the presence of some one to whom she could communicate her thoughts; and to whom could she so freely do so as those devoted friends?

They saw immediately on their entrance that she had met with something else to afflict her, and they eagerly inquired what it was.

With many tears Ethelinde related the conversation which had taken place in the morning, between her and her father, to which Kate and her mother listened with much interest and concern; and most deeply did they sympathize with her in the anxiety she must feel at the critical situation in which she was placed, from the melancholy facts —for after what he had so seriously asserted, that they were reluctantly compelled to receive as such—which Major Clarence had acknowledged to.

"Still," remarked Mrs. Rayborne, "I cannot, notwistanding all the seeming incontrovertible evidence which has been brought forward, bring my mind to believe in the criminality of your father, my dear Ethelinde. They have taken advantage of the weakness naturally consequent upon his late serious illness, but when the effects of that have happily become exhausted, he will be in a condition to repudiate the foul calumnies which I am satisfied Everard Welford and his father have brought against him, and to leave you to set all the threats of Everard at defiance, and to treat them with utter contempt."

Ethelinde shook her head mournfully. Fain would she have hoped as her excellent and amiable friend advised her to do, but reason told her that it was, at least, it would have been preposterous to have done so, after all that had taken place between her and her father, both previous and subsequent to his accident, and she therefore replied,—

"Alas! my dear friend, how much am I indebted to you for your kind attentions, your amiable, your generous efforts to inspire me with becoming fortitude and patience under my present severe trials; but, alas! I cannot think as you do; I feel that I have too much cause for apprehension; but believe me, which I know you will, when I declare, that the apprehension I feel for my own fate is trifling when put in comparison with that I experience for my beloved father. Oh, God! teach me how to act! I cannot look upon Everard Welford with any other sentiments than those of abhorence, and yet I am told, and my father confirms it that unless I consent to become the wife of the object of my disgust, and I must say, after his recent unmanly conduct towards me, of my detestation, I must consign him to an ignominious fate! Oh, Mrs. Rayborne; oh, Kate, my affectionate companion, Kate, whom I have ever looked upon with the ardent attachment of a sister, (a sentiment which I know has been and is reciprocated by you) how deeply must you commiserate with me in the sufferings I am now enduring, how sincerely must you sympathize with me in the peculiar, the extraordinary, the dreadful, and I may say, the almost unparalleled situation in which I find myself placed."

Sobs choked our lovely heroine's further utterance, and surely if Everard Welford could have seen her at that moment, his heart must have been moved to relent; bitterly insensible, notwithstanding as he appeared to be to all the better feelings of humanity, he must have reproached himself for the severe, the unwarrantable conduct he had hitherto pursued towards our heroine.

Kate Rayborne threw her fair arms around her sorrowing friend's neck, and their tears mingled together. Mrs. Rayborne stood by and gazed at them with the same intense emotion as if they had both been her daughters, and melancholy indeed was the silence which ensued, to allow them to give indulgence to the emotions that agitated their bosoms.

Mrs. Rayborne saw plainly, and it was with the deepest regret that she did, that there was too much reason in all the arguments which Ethelinde had advanced, and that they were unfortunately borne out too strongly by all the circumstances, especially in the corroborating statements of Mr. Clarence and Everard, for her to controvert them, and that conviction brought with it the most indescribable anguish, not only on account of Ethelinde and her father, but also on that of her son, whose hopes, she saw too plainly were doomed to be annihilated, and the anguish she felt at that moment could not have been surpassed by that which was raging within Ethelinde's own bosom.

"My dear girl," said the excellent woman, "I am certain that you are, as you say thoroughly convinced that there are no two individuals in the world who can and do more deeply sympathize with you in your misfortunes, than me and my daughter; but still we must not suffer ourselves to yield entirely to despair, or it will be giving your persecutor an advantage, which, depend upon it, he will not fail to avail himself of. Even should the Welfords really possess the terrible power which they profess to do over your's and your father's destiny, they cannot surely venture to go to the extreme which Everard you say has threatened."

"Not venture, my dear madam," sighed our heroine, "alas! what right have I to expect for a moment that they will act with the least degree of forbearance, after the bold, the daring, the insolent, and I may add, brutal language which Everard has recently made use of towards me? He has taken no pains to conceal from me that he is determined, and my heart's fears and predictions assure me that I have everything to apprehend from him. Has not my poor father confirmed his terrible assertion; namely, that his liberty, nay his very life, is in the hands of him and his father, and that unless I consent to sacrifice my hand, my liberty, all my brightest formed hopes, to Everard Welford, his fate is sealed, and that no earthly power can rescue him from it? Oh, God! surely these dreadful convictions are sufficient to drive even the most strong-minded person to madness."

Again our heroine covered her face with her hands, and sobbed as if her heart would break. It was in vain, for some time, that Kate and her mother endeavoured to impart some consolation to her. Her fate was such an extraordinary, and peculiar one, that it seemed not to admit of the least particle of hope or comfort, and they were indeed at a loss what argument to adduce to achieve so desirable an effect.

The form of Norman also, the last words he had uttered at the seventh tree in the dell, the solemn vow she had there plighted to him, a vow made in the face of Heaven, and which it would be worse than blasphemy to violate; all were impressed upon the memory of Ethelinde in such vivid characters, that they nearly overwhelmed her with their influence, and she felt at that trying moment as if death would have been a blissful release to her from sufferings which would certainly be more than her strength could endure.

And had she not acted criminally in granting that secret assignation which had led to such results ? In spite of all her endeavours to the contrary, she could not help reproaching herself with it, and she dreaded, yet had made up her mind to make her father acquainted with the whole truth. What could she expect but his keenest reproaches, for the want of duty and of confidence which she imagined he would consider she had shown towards him? And how terrible would be his anguish when he should learn the rash promise she had made to Norman; and yet she felt thoroughly convinced that he esteemed her lover almost as warmly as she did herself, and had he not unfortunately been so fettered, would gladly have hailed him for a son-in-law, certain that it would have been the means of promoting and consummating the happiness of a daughter whom he loved far more fondly than he did any other being in existence; whose life was far more precious to him than that of his own.

Mrs. Rayborne and her daughter could partly judge from the expressive countenance of Ethelinde, the thoughts which at that moment were passing in her mind, and which they could not fail to duly appreciate, but they did not offer to interrupt her for several moments, satisfied as they were that the indulgence of them would afford her some relief.

"Come, my dear Ethelinde," at last ejaculated Mrs. Rayborne, "you must still not give yourself up entirely to despair, for I am satisfied, indeed I cannot divest my mind of the conviction that the fears you now entertain will ere long be dissipated, and that something will occur to release you from the dangers with which you are at present threatened. One thing I have to make you acquainted with, which I am certain will afford you satisfaction."

"Oh, name it—name it!" eagerly demanded our heroine, "anything that can give me the least reasonable room for hope under my present torturing afflictions must afford me the most infinite gratification and consolation."

"Everard Welford," began Mrs. Rayborne. At the mention of his name Ethelinde's heart sank within her, but yet, coupled in the way it was with the observations of Mrs. Rayborne, she could not but feel her apprehensions almost immediately dissipated, and she eagerly demanded—

"Oh! what of him? Oh, tell me."

"I have been given to understand, from the most unquestionable authority," answered Mrs. Rayborne, "that the business which Everard Welford has gone upon will probably detain him for some weeks, so that you will at least be released from his importunities during that time, and in the meanwhile something may occur to alter your present painful circumstances altogether."

"Oh, thank Heaven for this intelligence," most fervently ejaculated our heroine, "and may it also, in the meantime, bring Everard and his father to relent in their unfeeling persecution. But are you certain that the information you have received, my dear madam, may be relied on?"

"Oh, yes," replied Mrs. Rayborne, I had it from those who have every means of knowing, and who would not misrepresent facts. During the absence of Everard, I would earnestly persuade you, Ethelinde, to endeavour to fortify your mind, and by that means you will strengthen the courage and resolution of your father, and enable him to combat with the artifices of his and your bitter enemies, and in all probability, however dark the aspect of affairs may at present appear to be, enable you both ultimately to triumph over them, and set them at defiance. I cannot, I will not believe that your father has ever been guilty to the extent which has been represented."

"Alas! has he not acknowledged it himself?" sighed Ethelinde, "Has he not admitted the truth of all that Everard Welford has alleged against him? That he has been guilty of ——. Oh, I cannot, I dare not give utterance to the dreadful word."

Mrs. Rayborne knew not what answer to make, for indeed the truth, the fatal truth appeared too painfully obvious to admit of doubt. It was opposed to all reason to imagine that Major Clarence would accuse himself of a crime which would deprive him of his liberty, and brand him with the name of a felon, unless there was some truth in the charge which had been brought against him, and notwithstanding all her efforts to comfort Ethelinde, and to inspire her with hope, she could not help, really, within herself apprehending the worst ultimate consequences.

"Let us banish all such gloomy thoughts, Ethelinde," she said at last, "and trust to Providence for the best."

"To-morrow," returned Ethelinde, "My poor father has promised to divulge everything; and need I say with what anxiety I await the arrival of that time? But from the fearful, the ominous prelude he has given me to the disclosure, have I not every reason to apprehend the worst? God help me! for I feel convinced that far more severe and dreadful trials than any I have hitherto experienced are yet in store for me, and never, after what I have already endured, shall I be able to find strength to support them."

"Put your trust in the Most High, my sweet girl;" again remarked Mrs. Rayborne, "and depend upon it that He will never forsake you in the hour of need."

"Heaven knows," solemnly and energetically returned Ethelinde, "that I have and do endeavour to do so. But if I display unwonted weakness, tell me, my dear friend, is there not, under such extraordinary and heart-rending circumstances, every excuse for it?"

"I admit, I admit that there is."

"Can it be wondered at that I should evince so much emotion after the dreadful charge of him who *demands* my hand, and the avowal of my unhappy father, of the truth of his accusation?"

"Indeed," answered Mrs. Rayborne, "I am compelled to admit that it is too true. But still I must once more urge upon you the absolute necessity, not only for your own sake, but that of your father, to make a powerful effort to struggle with your feelings, and you will yet pass triumphant through the fearful ordeal."

Many more observations passed between the friends, all tending to the same melancholy but praiseworthy object, and at length Kate and her mother took their leave, impressed with the hope that their wishes would not be entirely doomed to disappointment, although the account which Ethelinde had given them of what had taken place at the interview between her and her father, had, naturally enough, very much shocked and afflicted them, deeply as they were interested in the welfare and happiness of all parties concerned.

But that Major Clarence should have become so entangled in the meshes of Mr. Welford and his son—that he should be so completely in their power as to be in constant dread of them, and compelled to do their bidding even to the sacrifice of his lovely daughter to one whom she could now only thoroughly hate and despise, was a mystery which she found it utterly impossible to solve. Nor could she bring her mind to believe in the truth of the guilty charge which had been brought against him, and which it seemed, he had himself admitted. It was too monstrous, too strongly opposed to all that she had ever known of him to be entertained.

She had enjoyed the pleasure of his friendship for a long series of years, and never during that period had she known him guilty of a single act which did not reflect the highest credit upon his character as a man and gentleman. He was universally esteemed by all who knew him, both high and low, rich and poor, and she knew of no one that would have been bold enough to have ventured to impeach his honour and integrity; therefore was it that the present circumstance was the more impenetrable and irreconcilable, and she awaited with the greatest anxiety until it was fully explained.

"Alas, my dear mother," said Kate, as they pursued their way home; "how sincerely do I pity poor Ethelinde and her father. I fear indeed that this is but the prelude to the dreadful ruin which seems about to burst upon their heads. Were there not some truth in the statement of Everard Welford, it does not seem probable that Mr. Clarence would have himself acknowledged it, or have been in such dread of him and his father. Indeed it will be more, much more than the strength of Ethelinde will be able to combat against; and my dear brother too · what will be his anguish when he comes to hear of it, and to find that his hopes are all annihilated at one fell blow?"

Mrs. Rayborne sighed.

"For Heaven's sake, Kate," she said, "do not let us anticipate such dreadful things. I cannot believe that Providence will be so unmerciful as to visit the innocent with such unmerited sufferings. No, no, child, we shall see Ethelinde Clarence happy, depend upon it, and blest in the hallowed love of the man of her choice, my beloved Norman, whom may Heaven protect from every danger, and quickly restore him to our arms."

Most heartily did Kate respond to this prayer, and in a few minutes more they arrived at home.

No sooner had Mrs. Rayborne and her daughter departed from the mansion, than Ethelinde, having struggled hard to tranquillise her feelings, and succeeded much better than she had been at first led to hope, hastened to the chamber of her father, anxious to know how he was.

She found him awake, and looking much better and more composed than she had expected, and to her eager inquiries, he replied that he was perfectly free from pain.

"Oh, thank God for that!" fervently cried the poor girl, pressing her father's hand to her lips, and raising her wearied eyes towards Heaven; "may you speedily be restored to health and happiness."

"Happiness! ah, no!" sighed Mr. Clarence, and he ominously shook his head, while Ethelinde felt a pang shoot through her heart which was torturing in the extreme.

"But," resumed Mr. Clarence, appearing suddenly to recollect himself and changing his tone, "you look pale, ill, and fatigued, my poor child. Retire to your chamber, and endeavour to obtain some repose. To-morrow will be a day of trial to you, which it will require all your fortitude to sustain. Good night, my darling Ethelinde, and may Heaven bless you, and watch over, and protect you from all the dangers with which you are unhappily surrounded."

Ethelinde embraced her father, who pressed his lips tenderly upon her fair forehead, and then with a melancholy and foreboding heart, she slowly retired from the room, and sought the solitude of her own apartment.

The morrow, the important morrow, so anxiously looked forward to, yet so dreaded, what would it reveal? This was the thought which held a predominant place in the mind of Ethelinde; every other feeling, every other subject was totally absorbed by it, and yet she shuddered with irrepressible dread and the most terrible presentiments as she dwelt upon it. What fearful story was she destined to hear from the lips of her unfortunate father? For that it was of the most dreadful description she could not doubt, after what he had said; and how could she ever find strength sufficient to support the shock it would be certain to inflict upon her feelings? She sunk upon her knees, and fervently she offered up her prayers to Heaven to give her that courage to combat with any of the fearful dangers which she anticipated were in store for her.

The important morning arrived! Ethelinde arose from her couch, on which she had passed a sleepless night, and with the assistance of Jane, having dressed herself, awaited with the utmost anxiety and trepidation the summons to the breakfast table.

"How pale you look, miss," remarked Jane, "I am afraid you are very ill, and really instead of your going down stairs, you seem to be more fit to return to bed. Dear me, what anguish it will cause my master to see you in such a condition."

"Have you seen my father this morning, Jane?" asked our heroine, little heeding what she said in respect to her own personal appearance.

"Yes, miss," answered Jane.

"And how did he appear, Jane?"

"Better, miss, than I have seen him for some time," replied Jane, "and he was quite cool and collected."

"Thank Heaven for that," earnestly ejaculated Ethelinde; "may the Almighty assist us both through this dreadful trial, and defeat the machinations of our enemies."

Ethelinde having completed her toilette, once more sat herself down in her chair, and gave way to the melancholy thoughts and presentiments which, in spite of all endeavours to the contrary crowded upon her mind. She was now, then, about to hear a recital, which, according to her father's own admission must convict him of a crime, the most injurious towards his fellow-creatures. She must listen to a statement of facts, which, independent of the poignant regret they must cause her, must consign her to despair, to indescribable misery; and from which she could only escape by resigning her beloved parent into the hands of justice, and condemning him to an ignominious fate !

What a dreadful situation was she placed in, and there were no means whatever, of her escaping from it. She trembled to meet her parent, and to hear from his lips, the acknowledgement of his guilt, notwithstanding what Jane had said respecting his being so cool and collected; and fain would she have postponed the disclosure, notwithstanding her eagerness to become acquainted with the painful particulars.

As these thoughts were passing in her mind, a servant entered the room, and informed her that her father awaited her presence at the breakfast table. With a melancholy heart, but at the same time attempting to assume all the composure that she possibly could, she descended to the apartment in which the morning repast was provided.

Her father was seated on her entrance, and although his countenance was naturally pale, from the effects of his recent accident, his demeanour generally speaking, was, as Jane had represented it to be, cool and collected, and in fact, she was astonished to behold it, after what had occured on the two previous days.

Mr. Clarence arose immediately on the entrance of his daughter, and advancing towards her, took her hand, looked with all a father's fondness in her countenance, and led her to a seat.

"My dear father," cried the affectionate girl, "how it gladdens my heart to see you looking so composed. God grant that it may be the augury of future happiness."

Major Clarence embraced our heroine in silence, and a tear of parental fondness and sympathy in the sufferings—in the dreadful anxiety and suspense—he knew perfectly well she must at that mo-

ment be enduring, fell upon her cheek.

"You are pale, child," he said, "I fear you have had but little sleep, and that your mind is in no condition to hear the fearful particulars of that which it is now indispensably necessary I should impart to you."

"Oh, no, my beloved father," replied Ethelinde, trying to assume a courage which she did not in reality feel, "indeed you labour under a misapprehension. I am fully prepared to listen to your explanation, for I feel fully satisfied that you will by it, stand perfectly exonerated from the foul aspersions which have been cast upon your character."

"Oh, no! oh, no!" exclaimed Mr. Clarence with a burst of agony, "would to Heaven, my sweet, my beautiful girl, for your sake, that I could rebut the guilty charge which has been brought against me. But I cannot. The time has arrived for the fearful disclosure, and my conscience tells me that I should be doubly culpable, that I should be an hypocrite of the worst description, if I longer withheld it from you. Oh, God, how frightfully, but still how justly am I now punished for having offended your laws. This degradation in the eyes of my own child, is terrible, but still I feel it as a just retribution for the offences of which I have been guilty."

"Oh, my father," cried the horror-struck Ethelinde, "for the love of Heaven do not thus, unjustly, I am satisfied reproach yourself. You cannot, you are not, deserving of it."

"Ethelinde," replied her father, in solemn accents, "I am unworthy of your commiseration. I am a villain, a monstrous villain !"

"Forbear ! forbear !"

"'Tis too true ! Oh, Ethelinde what a tale of horror and guilt will you have to listen to. Would to God that it had pleased him to take me to himself before I could have shocked your ears by repeating it to you."

"Gracious Heaven!" exclaimed our heroine, with a burst of emotion which the reader may imagine, but no language can describe, "for what am I reserved? My dear father, let me not hear the dreadful story at all, if it thus involves your happiness and your honour."

"You must hear it, Ethelinde," returned Major Clarence; "it is necessary that you should hear it to understand how it is that I have sold you; aye, sold you, girl, and that, I now have reason to fear, to a villain of the blackest chaacte-."

"For the love of God, my dear fa-ther," again implored Ethelinde, "do not talk thus."

"My poor child, I talk as reason and truth guide me. But compose yourself, Ethelinde, I beseech you, my dear Ethelinde, and partake of the morning repast, and then try to muster all the fortitude

MRS. RAYBORNE'S INTERVIEW WITH EVERARD WELFORD.

you can to listen to that which I have to state to you. You have already been prepared for the nature of it, and after what has transpired between you and Everard Welford, it is necessary that I should make you acquainted with all the painful particulars. It is better that you should hear it from my lips than his."

Ethelinde fixed upon her unfortunate father a look which penetrated to his heart, and endeavoured to comply with his request; but the repast remained almost untouched by either of them, and a dreary silence of several minutes ensued, during which interval, Major Clarence seemed to be trying to collect his thoughts, and to fortify himself for the painful task he had imposed upon himself; while our heroine was all trembling anxiety, yet dreaded him to begin. The warning he had given her, left her not the least reasonable room for hope, and her fate was presented to her as clearly as if it had been reflected to her in a mirror.

"My dear girl," at length began Mr. Clarence, in a loud and particularly agitated and impressive tone of voice, "I am about to withdraw the curtain from the unfortunate and guilty scenes of my past life, and in doing so, I need not tell you the bitter anguish and remorse it will cost me, more especially as upon you, my poor child, will rest the principal punishment for the offences I have committed, unless you sacrifice me to the malice and revenge of my enemies, which, in truth, is no more than I deserve, and————"

"Oh, no, no, no;" eagerly interrupted Ethelinde, "say not so, my dear father, for it shocks my ears to hear it. Oh, what have I ever done that you should form so ungenerous an estimate of the duty and affection I feel I owe, and ought to owe, towards you? Nothing, oh, there is nothing, God knows, there is no sacrifice, however dreadful it may be, that I will hesitate to make, to save my father from the fate which he anticipates. Nay, even if my life is required for his salvation, it is at his command."

My noble girl;" cried Mr. Clarence, embracing her with a burst of the most fervent emotion, "how little do I deserve such generous devotion as this. But—but, let me at once get over the dreadful task allotted to me. Ethelinde, you have confessed (and I needed not your acknowledgement of the fact to convince me of it), that you love Norman Rayborne?"

"Father," replied the maiden, and her heart palpitated more violently than before; "that question, I humbly presume, needs no reply from me. Norman Rayborne is worthy, he is good, he is honourable; he has acknowledged to me that he loves me, and—why should I deny it—my heart beats responsive with his own."

"And Everard Welford holds no place in that heart, Ethelinde?"

"He once did in my esteem, my dear father, but I now can only look upon him with fear and disgust."

"Oh, God! oh, God!" groaned Mr. Clarence, beating his breast, "what misery and injustice have my crimes been productive of. Ethelinde, though I am your father, you should turn from me with loathing and disgust."

"Oh, my dear father," cried our heroine, looking in his countenance with the most earnest emotion, "you surely cannot know what you say."

"Alas, I do, my deeply injured child," returned Major Clarence, "would to God that I was indeed unconscious to everything. Norman Rayborne has got such firm possession of your affections, that nothing can displace him?"

"Nothing but his unfaithfulness;—which I believe him to be incapable of."

"Can you not cease to think of him in any other character than that of a friend?" eagerly demanded Mr. Clarence.

"Never! never!" energetically replied Ethelinde;—"Even though Norman Rayborne should deceive me, and place his affections upon another, he, and he alone, must ever possess my love."

"Alas! alas!" sighed Mr. Clarence, "then is my misery indeed complete. Ethelinde, tell me, have any vows passed between you and this young man? Have you pledged yourself in any way to him!"

Ethelaide trembled, and the deepest blushes suffused her cheeks. The question was one that she had anticipated would be put to her, but which she was by no means prepared to answer; however, she saw that it was impossible to evade it, and she threw herself on her knees at her father's feet, while the powerful emotions which struggled in her breast, for a few moments quite choked her utterance.

Major Clarence raised his lovely daughter, and pressed her affectionately to his bosom, as he observed;—

"I see it all, my poor child; and doubly wretched do I feel that I should be the guilty means of marring happiness so well merited."

"My dear father," said Ethelinde, "I implore your pardon, for having for the first time acted in disobedience to your will"

She then, in a tremulous voice, revealed to him the whole truth, to which he listened with the most unmitigated feelings of anguish; but, as a sudden thought seemed to flash upon his brain, he exclaimed;—

"Three years you say, Ethelinde, was the time specified between you and Norman Rayborne, for the fulfilment of the compact?"

Etherlinde egerly answered in the affirmative.

"'Tis well," said Mr. Clarence, with a look of satisfaction, "who knows what may transpire in that time?—Could I only persuade Mr. Welford and his son to await that time—"

"Oh, do, my dear father, endeavour to do so;" fervently supplicated Ethelinde, "and all may yet be well."

"And yet I fear from Everard's recent conduct," remarked Mr. Clarence, "that he will remain inflexible. But should he even yield compliance to such a proposal, he would certainly expect and demand that you should receive his addresses during that period, Ethelinde."

"Alas! alas!" sighed our heroine, "how can I do so?—My feelings revolt from the bare idea, and after the recent unfeeling and unmanly conduct he has evinced towards me, I fear that I can scarcely treat him with common respect."

"For your own sake, my poor child, said Mr. Clarence. "You see that we have no other means of effecting that object, in which both our happiness and our future prospects are so deeply, so immediately in fact, involved."

"Alas! my father, I cannot hold out any such promise."

"Then it is useless to appeal to Everard Welford or his father."

"But he cannot force his addresses upon me against my will, and your inclination, father," returned Ethelinde.

"Ah, Ethelinde!" sighed Mr. Clarence, "have I not before repeatedly told you that Everard Welford holds me in his power? That my liberty, my life, are in his hands?"

"Oh, it cannot be!" ejaculated our heroine, with a shudder.

"It is, alas, too true," returned Mr. Clarence, solmnly; "but listen while I reveal to you the long hidden secret, and then judge for yourself."

The moment, the important moment had now arrived, which should elucidate that subject, in which the whole happiness of our heroine was involved. She trembled, and even anxious as she was to hear the painful revelation, she would most gladly have spared her father the anguish, the torture of mind. which must occur to him under the circumstances.

"Come closer to me, child," said the major, "and do not sympathize with me until you hear the plain statement of facts which I shall give to you. My dear Ethelinde, I have before stated to you that the indiscretions of which I have been guilty, sprang entirely from my own imprudence; I will not attempt for a moment to exonerate my character, from that serious, that ominous charge, nor to implicate my present persecutor in the first spring (if I may so call it), of my criminal career."

"Oh, my father," interrupted Ethelinde, with a burst of agony, "apply not such harsh, such unjustifiable terms, I am convinced, to your conduct. My father could never have been wilfully criminal. You reproach yourself too severely; you act uncharitably towards yourself."

"My sweetest child, my gentle Ethelinde," replied her father, "would that your opinion were correct; what misery and shame should both of us then be spared. But it is you, my dear girl, that act too generously towards me. Oh, how unworthy am I of your consideration."

"Father, you torture me to madness by thus cruelly, and I cannot help thinking, unjustly accusing yourself of that which I cannot believe you to have been guilty."

"Again my poor child, I implore you to endeavour to compose your feelings, and to listen patiently and attentively to the painful, the guilty story I have to reveal."

"Let me not hear it, father," said Ethelinde, "if indeed, the facts you have to disclose, shall criminate yourself, rather let me remain in ignorance of them for ever."

"No, no, Ethelinde," returned Mr. Clarence, hastily, and with much emotion, "that must not be. It is necessary that you should know the whole of the fearful facts, that you may be fully aware of the painful position in which your unfortunate father has placed you, and the power which Everard Welford holds over you and me. I have long wished to make you acquainted with the dreadful facts, but could not find courage to do so. However, the crisis has now arrived, when secresy can no longer be maintained. Everard Welford claims your hand, and unless you grant it to him, your father must be sacrificed to his vengeance and disappointment. Oh, would that my late accident had proved fatal, for, then would you have been released from this terrible obligation. Ethelinde, I repeat, that I am totally unworthy of your sympathy. By my crimes I have blasted all your prospects of happiness, and sold you to one whom I now am convinced is a heartless scoundrel. Ethelinde, you should look upon me with abhorrence instead of reverence. Oh, that I had died! oh, that I had died!"

The poor old man again covered his face with his hands, and sobbed as if his heart would break. Ethelinde went to him—she threw her arms round his neck—she impressed warm kisses of affection upon his venerable cheeks, but so powerful were the feelings which struggled in her breast that she could not utter a word.

Another pause ensued, during which, both father and daughter gave unrestrained indulgence to the torrent of agonizing feelings which agitated both their bosoms.

"Oh, my dear father," at length our heroine found strength sufficient to ejaculate; "do not, I beseech you, give utterance to such dreadful observations, condemnatory of yourself, and of which I feel satisfied you are undeserving. Reserve your explanation to some future period, when your recruited strength will better enable you to give it, and——"

"No, no, Ethelinde," interrupted her father; "there must be no further delay. Everard Welford demands your hand, and his recent conduct towards you shows that he is determined to enforce the fulfilment of the fatal compact, into which I entered many years since with his father, and you must be already acquainted with all the fearful particulars, so that you may be enabled to meet him in a proper spirit, and to judge of the diference which is due from you to me. But a few moments allow me, my child, while I collect my thoughts, and then listen patiently to me while I unburthen my mind of that which has for years pressed upon it with a weight of lead."

Etheline fixed upon her father a look of the most unbounded affection and sympathy, but she returned no answer. Mr. Clarence shuddered under her glances, and averted his looks, sighing deeply at the same time. How bitter, how overpowering was the remorse, and the self-reproach that he, at that moment experienced. The fond attachment and confidence, the generous commiseration of his amiable and lovely daughter, was dreadful punishment to him, more terrible, because his conscience told him how totally unworthy he was of that poor girl's pity or forbearance. He had sacrificed her, he had annihilated all her young hopes, made a desert of that which might have been all luxuriant in bliss; and, could he, therefore, look upon himself in any other character than that of a murderer? He could not! And, therefore, did he tremble in the presence of his deeply injured daughter.

Ethelinde's heart throbbed violently against her side during this brief silence, and little was she prepared to hear the painful facts which it was too evident her father had to disclose. Rather, much rather, would she, that they could have been burried in oblivion for ever. Mentally, but fervently, did she offer up her prayers to the Almighty, to avert the evils which she had too much reason to apprehend were in store for her, and to give her father strength to make the explanation he had imposed upon himself, at the same time, that she trusted that the facts would not turn out to be so bad as he had represented them, but that he had allowed his fears to exaggerate them.

At length, after a violent struggle with his feelings, Major Clarence looked up much more calmly than might have been expected, and beckoning Ethelinde to him, when she had taken a seat by his side, he remarked:

"My darling Ethelinde, this is a weakness which I ought and will conquer. The time has arrived for the truth to be disclosed, and any maudlin sentimentality on my part is, to say the least of it, very ill-becoming. I am placed upon my trial, and justly so; I plead guilty, and it is for me to endeavour to make all the atonement in my power, for the transgressions of which I have been guilty. You, my child, are the victim, the innocent victim of those transgressions, and it behoves me to make a full and ample confession of the injuries I have done you, that you may be placed in a position to judge of the mercy and forbearance you ought to extend towards me. I claim none, I feel myself unworthy of it, and, therefore do I hope you will rather resist the importunities of Everard Welford, though I become the victim in consequence, than sacrifice yourself to a man whom you must not only detest, but despise."

"Father, dear father," ejaculated our heroine, with the greatest emotion, "I cannot bear to hear you talk thus. You do, you must unjustly reproach yourself. What can you ever have done, that you should have to make atonement to me, your child?"

"Listen, Ethelinde," replied her father, solemnly, but in a firmer tone of voice than he had before been able to assume, "and judge for yourself. The melancholy story I have to communicate is brief, but do not interrupt me during the progress of it, harrowing as I am fully aware it will be to your feelings, or I shall not have the fortitude to complete it. I should have revealed it years ago, but I could never find resolution to do so, and I had indulged the hope that Everard Welford would have proved himself worthy of, and have won your affections, or have fixed his mind upon some other damsel; in which case, the fulfilment of the fatal vow, exacted from me by his father, would never have been urged, and the guilty past might have been buried in oblivion. But, unfortunately, such has not turned out to be the case, and I should become doubly criminated were I, any longer, to remain silent. And yet, Ethelinde,

need I tell you how keenly, how poignantly, I feel the cruel necessity of thus being compelled to degrade myself in the eyes of my own child? To——"

"Oh, it is impossible, my dear father," interrupted Ethelinde, with a burst of the most inexpressible anguish, "that you should ever have done that which can degrade you in my eyes or that of any other individual. You, that have ever been so kind, so affectionate, so indulgent to me, to whom all who have the happiness of knowing you, however lofty or humble may be their station, look up with esteem and reverence. I cannot, I will not believe it."

"Ethelinde," exclaimed Mr. Clarence, "this generous confidence, so ill-merited, tortures me more than all. I could better endure your reproaches than these marks of your devoted attachment. You have told me of the crime of which Everard Welford has accused me?"

"But it is not true; it cannot be; it must be a foul, a base, a malicious calumny!"

"Would to God that it was, my child;" groaned Mr. Clarence, striking his forehead with the intensity of his emotion; "would to God that I could rebut that fearful charge, then would there be no necessity for my being placed in the degrading, the painful position in which I now am. But I plead guilty; I acknowledge myself to have criminally offended against Mr. Welford; I am entirely at his mercy, and if I break the vow which in your infancy I made to him, I shall be at once delivered up to the laws of my country, and my fate is certain."

"Oh, God! can this be?" cried the distracted Ethelinde; "oh, if it is, would that it had pleased Heaven to take me to itself ere I could have arrived at the knowledge of the dreadful facts."

"Say rather that it had pleased the Almighty to shorten my days," ejaculated her father fervently, "then would you have been released from the dangers by which you are at present surrounded, my child. But this is a waste of time and words. Listen to me Ethelinde, while I recount, in as few words as possible, the melancholy facts connected with my indiscretions, if I dare apply so mild a term to offences that have been productive of such fatal consequences."

"Oh my father," replied Ethelinde, "let me not hear them, if the recital will cost you so much agony as your observations imply."

"You must hear them, child," replied Mr. Clarence, vehemently; "your whole future happiness, your every hope depends upon the revelation, and I should be worse than criminal, if I any longer withheld it. Besides, it will relieve my mind from a burthen which has become too torturing for me any longer to endure."

Ethelinde returned no answer, and Major Clarence remained silent for a minute or two; during this time all the melancholy events of the past were evidently passing in painful review before his mind. At length he took his daughter's hand within his own, and looking in her face with the most unutterable affection, said :—

"My dear Ethelinde, I know I need not remind you of the eminent virtues of your sainted mother; that gentle, that amiable being, whose whole life was devoted to the performance of benevolent and Christian actions."

Tears gushed from the eyes of our heroine, as she replied :—

"Oh, my father, can I ever cease to remember and to adore the memory of that best of parents and of women? When I cease to do so, which is impossible, may Heaven forsake me!"

Major Clarence enfolded his lovely daughter to his bosom, and imprinted a fervent kiss upon her lips, and it was some moments ere the power of his emotions would allow him to resume; but at length he did so in the following words :—

"Ah, Ethelinde, your mother was indeed all that was virtuous, good, and estimable, and yet she could not win the regard of every one. My mother, for instance, entertained a most unaccountable prejudice against her, and so far influenced my father, who unfortunately was not without his weak points, that he not only refused his sanction to my paying my addresses to your mother, but commanded me to banish her from my memory, on pain of his eternal displeasure.

"But was it possible that such an act of parental tyranny could ever dissever two hearts that were so fondly and indissolubly united?—Oh, no it could not, and after in vain, remonstrating with my parents, I determined in spite of the consequences which might ensue, that no other than Ethelinde Winstanley should ever become my wife. From childhood we had been pledged to each other; she was my equal both by birth and station, in point of intrinsic merits. I felt myself unworthy of her, and, therefore, was I fully resolved that no consideration should compel me to submit to such an arbitrary act of injustice. Again I repeated my solemn vows of constancy to your mother, Ethelinde, and we swore that unless we became united, to ever remain single. We then parted, and I returned to college.

"On my leaving the university, I chose the profession of arms, and having purchased an ensigncy, joined my regiment, which shortly afterwards received orders for Flanders.

"The anguish of your mother at the prospect of a separation, and the uncertainty of our ever meeting again, may be readily imagined, and my agony was equal to her own. Again I threw myself at my parents' feet, and implored of them to give their consent to the celebration of our nuptials, previous to my departure from my native land, but an inexorable rejection was the only answer I received; could I do anything else than reject in my turn, such cruel, such unreasonable, and unjust coercion? —I tried every argument that affection to your mother, Ethelinde, and duty to my parents sugested, without effect, and when I found that fail, I considered myself justified in breaking through the parental trammels, which had been placed upon me. I considered myself bound in the face of Heaven to your mother, my dearest Ethelinde, and nothing would induce me to sacrifice her or myself to the false prejudices and caprices of my parents.

"We were privately married, and when my father was apprised of the fact, which I took the earliest opportunity to do, as he had promised, or more properly speaking, threatened, he discarded me; refused to see either me or your mother, Ethelinde, and told me in a brief and cruel note that henceforward we must be as strangers to each other. Sorry am I to say that my mother coincided in that severe condemnation, and I found myself at once thrown upon the world without the natural resources I had an undoubted right to expect.

"Heaven pardon my parents for this act of cruelty and injustice, for from that I have every reason to date the misfortunes, the indiscretions, and evils that occurred to me.

"My wife's father was unfortunately at the time engaged in a law-suit, which ended fatally for him, and the consequence was, from his being placed in a state of more than affluence, he was reduced to comparative beggary. Consequently, my dear child, you may judge of the awkward position in which your mother and myself found ourselves placed.

"As I have before stated, my regiment was immediately ordered abroad, and my wife, my beloved, my devoted wife accompanied me, ill as she was prepared, both from physical and mental indisposition to undertake such a hazardous and trying expedition. I wrote my parents a farewell epistle on my quitting my native shores, remonstrating with them on the harshness of their conduct towards me and that amiable being whom I had made my wife, and they added to their injustice (for such is the only term which I can apply to it), by returning my letter unopened.

"Under these painful circumstances, my wife and me left England, without property or, at least, more than my humble commission produced, and thus did we struggle on for months, exposed to every privation and vicissitude which such a calamity (if I may so term it, for it must be a calamity where your parents' hearts are unjustly closed against you), must naturally produce. We murmured not; we bore our misfortunes with fortitude, and, I speak it without egotism, it was the rectitude of our own consciences that enabled us to do so."

"But I was poor, very poor. My poor wife's father also (although his will was good) was unable to render us the least assistance, and my pride, my honest pride, would not allow me to apply to my father, after the manner in which he had discarded me. Oh, God! would that the authors of my being had not so much to answer for, but it is to them, and them alone, I can justly attribute all the errors of which I have been guilty."

Mr. Clarence was compelled to pause, for his emotions were too powerful to allow him to proceed. Ethelinde had listened to him hitherto with the utmost agitation, and deeply were her sympathies aroused, but now her feelings were more than ever excited, when she saw the cruel injustice with which her father had been treated by his own parents.

A silence of some minutes ensued, during which interval the father and daughter gave free indulgence to the emotions which agitated their bosoms.

"I must proceed with my melancholy narrative," at length resumed Major Clarence, "but doubtless, my dear child, you can and do fully appreciate the feelings I must naturally experience in recalling these torturing circumstances to my memory."

"Oh, my poor father," ejaculated our heroine, throwing her arms around her parent's neck, "why need you dwell upon that painful subject? — Defer your revelation to some future occasion."

"No, Ethelinde," replied her father, "it has been deferred too long; but all must be, and I am determined shall now be, explained.

"In the first engagement I was very severely wounded, and then, if I had needed it, I received full evidence of the unbounded affection your mother bore towards me. Oh, how solicitously did she attend me; with what anxious care did she administer to my wants, what anguish did she suffer during my indisposition, and how great was her delight on my restoration to convalescence?

"Arthur Welford and I had been fellow collegians. I believed him to be my friend. He had formerly paid his addresses to your mother, Ethelinde, but finding that I was the chosen of her heart, he honourably as I then imagined, withdrew his suit, and left the field open to me. Little did I then know the deceptive part he was playing. Little did I suspect the scheme of vengeance that he nurtured in his bosom; that it was he who had been the primary cause of poisoning the minds of my parents against me and my wife, or I should probably have escaped the evils, the misfortunes I have now such bitter cause to lament. Oh, he was a most wily hypocrite, and severely have I suffered from being drawn into his snares.

"It was just after my recovery from the wound to which I have alluded, that I and Arthur Welford met, after a separation of several years. He evinced the greatest pleasure at seeing me again, and I, believing in his sincerity, expressed and felt no less gratification. Towards my wife he showed the most marked respect, congratulated her on the choice she had made, and never, for a moment, offered the least allusion to his own former pretensions. There could not be the least suspicion as to his sincerity, excited in the bosom of either myself or my wife, for, independent of the candour of his manner, he was united to a most amiable woman, and report said that they lived in the greatest state of harmony and happiness together. But little did I anticipate that he was, at that very moment, when he professed the most ardent and devoted friendship towards me, contemplating my destruction.

"I hesitated not to confide to him all the particulars of my situation, and while he strongly deprecated my father's conduct, he offered me with generosity, which, at the time, I believed to be almost unexampled, any pecuniary assistance I might require.

"I considered him a real friend, and, pressed as I was at the time, I did not scruple to avail myself of his offer, trusting that, in a short time my father would repent of his harsh conduct towards me, and that I should be enabled to repay Mr. Welford the sums which he had, as I, at that time imagined, so generously advanced me.

"Oh, could I but have conceived the base, the villainous plot, he was at that very time concocting against me, how thoroughly I should have despised and scouted him.

"The war over, we returned to England, when I once more threw myself at my father's feet, and supplicated his forgiveness. But he turned a deaf ear to me, and refused to recognise your mother as my wife.

"My father-in-law was greatly embarrassed, in fact, from the unfortunate issue of his law-suit, he was reduced almost to a state of beggary, and consequently, the limited salary I derived from my profession was all but useless, under the exigences of the case. I was again compelled to apply to Arthur Welford, and once more became his debtor for a large sum.

"About this period Mrs. Welford gave birth to a son, the present Everard, the claimaint of your hand, Ethelinde, and only three months afterwards you, my child, were born.

"Mr. Welford pretended to bring about a reconciliation between me and my father, but at the very time, as I have since discovered, he was misrepresenting not only my conduct but that of your amiable mother to him, and making it appear that we were both carrying on a career of shame which, if it had been true, ought to have stamped us with eternal obloquy."

"Oh, God! my father," exclaimed our heroine, "is it possible that Mr. Welford could ever have been such a villain."

"He has, Ethelinde," answered Mr. Clarence, "believe me I do not exaggerate in what I am stating to you. Placing every confidence in his professions, I looked upon him as my best friend, and hesitated not to continue to receive his assistance, satisfied as I was that my father would not carry the animosity he at present displayed towards me to the grave, and that I should be able to repay him at some future period for all the kindness he had shown towards me.

"So grateful did I feel towards him for the friendship, the disinterested friendship, as I imagined, he had evinced for me, that I knew not what return to make him as an acknowledgemen for the services he had rendered me.

"It was upon one occasion that we were conversing upon the probable future prospects of our children, should they arrive at years of maturity, that Mr. Welford suggested the fatal alliance between you, Ethelinde, and his son. I hailed the proposition with delight, forgetting at the time, the injustice of the arrangement, and that you might grow up dissimilar in tastes, in dispositions, and sentiments, and that by yielding my consent I was becoming guilty of the same species of parental tyranny, as that of which I had such ample reason to accuse my father and mother; blind, infatuated as I must have been at the time, to permit myself to be drawn into the snare which was so artfully laid to entrap me. Yes, Ethelinde, I sold you, cruelly, remorselessly sold to the parent of one, who has shewn himself to be a villain. That night I made a solemn vow, I entered into a fatal compact to the effect that if you lived to the years of maturity, and Everard Welford was willing, no other man but him

AGONY OF ETHELINDE ON HEARING RAYBORNE'S MISSION.

should make you his bride; and to the fulfillment of that rash oath, I afterwards bound myself in the most fearful manner Oh, Ethelinde, after this acknowledgement, although I am your father, can you help looking upon me, with any other feelings than those of disgust and horror?"

Mr. Clarence paused, overcome by the emotions which those thoughts caused, and Ethelinde was herself too much agitated to be able for a short time to make any reply. She saw at once the dreadful position in which her father was placed, the artful, demoniacal snare which had been laid to entrap him, and while she deeply commiserated with him in his misfortunes, she saw with terror the fate which threatened, and dreaded to hear the further particulars he had to divulge.

"Alas, my father," she at last said, "think not for a moment that I am going to reproach you for an act into which you was fatally ensnared by the deepest and blackest designing villany; but I cannot, I dare not believe that you are bound in any shape to fulfil a vow extorted under such circumstances, and especially when you find that Everard Welford cannot even possess my esteem."

"Alas! alas! my poor injured child," returned Major Clarence, "I have no alternative than either to fulfil that fatal vow, or to be denounced to the world and punished as a criminal. Everard Welford told you that him and his father held certain documents in their possession, which would fully establish my guilt, and that unless you yielded to his demands, I could not escape disgrace and punishment."

"He did! he did! but nevertheless I cannot, I will not believe it."

"Ethelinde, once more I solemnly declare that he spoke the truth, and that I am the guilty and unfortunate being he has represented me to be. Once more I tell you that I am totally unworthy of your sympathy, and so you must, in spite of your generous nature, consider, when you hear the conclusion of my melancholy narrative."

"My dear father," exclaimed Ethelinde, "I cannot patiently listen to your dreadful self-accusation. My father could never have been so guilty as he represents he has."

"My dear Ethelinde," replied her father, "need I assure you how agonizing it is to me to be thus compelled to shock and harden your feelings? How bitter is the remorse I experience at being thus forced to degrade myself in your eyes? But the truth must be told; —the time has arrived when it can no longer be concealed, and however severe the trial, and dreadful indeed it will be for me, I will not shrink from the task. Pray, my child, endeavour to compose yourself, and to hear me out."

"Father, dear father," replied our heroine, "as I have again and again observed, I implore you, rather than disclose that which is likely to cause you so much agony of mind, let it remain a secret from me for ever."

"That cannot be, my poor child," answered her agitated parent, "Everard Welford has already intimated, nay, boldly asserted the character of my offence to you, and has likewise threatened to publish it to the world, and, therefore, it is better that you should hear the melancholy and guilty facts from my lips than his, so that you may be placed in a proper position to judge how far your unfortunate parent is worthy of your pity, and likewise whether you should, in justice, sacrifice your own happiness or his liberty."

"Oh, my beloved parent," exclaimed the affectionate girl, throwing herself into her father's arms, and scarcely able to proceed from the violence of her emotion; "do no rack your daughter's heart by talking thus. There is no sacrifice that I would not willingly make to——"

She was interrupted by a tap at the door of the apartment in which this interview had taken place, and being desired to do so, a servant entered, and announced that Mr. Welford, senior, was waiting below, and demanded an immediate interview with Major Clarence.

Ethelinde's heart sunk within her, and she turned ghastly pale, when she heard the name of the father of the man she so much dreaded mentioned, and Mr. Clarence also evinced much agitation, but he speedily recovered himself, and addressing the servant, said,—

"Desire Mr. Welford to walk up stairs."

He then turned to his daughter, and embracing her, observed—

"I regret, my dear Ethelinde, that this interruption should have taken place at such a time, but perhaps, it may be all for the best. Retire, my child for a time; it is not meet that you should be present at this interview."

"Oh, my beloved father," replied his beauteous daughter, "would that it was over, for much do I dread the consequences of it. I am too fearful that any appeal you may make to Mr. Welford, after what you have stated, and the conduct of his son, will be of little or no avail; and how can I do otherwise than entertain the most gloomy and sensible apprehensions. God protect you, and grant that the melancholy presentiments which beset my mind may not be realised."

Her father kissed her affectionately, and with a look of encouragement, but at the same time without uttering a syllable. He pointed towards an opposite door, and Ethelinde with a deep sigh emerged from it, just as Mr. Welford entered at the other. With hesitating and agitated footsteps, she sought her own apartment, where throwing herself upon a sofa, she for some time was totally engrossed by the subjects which distracted her mind.

CHAPTER VII.

THE MEETING BETWEEN MAJOR CLARENCE AND MR. WELFORD.—THE APPEAL.—THE THREAT.

How agonizing were the reflections, how painful the suspense of Ethelinde during the time this interview between her father and Mr. Welford was taking place. She had heard quite enough from her parent's acknowledgement, and the threats of Everard, to lead her to apprehend the worst; and she looked forward to the result with the most awful, the most insupportable agony and anxiety. She could not for a moment flatter herself (after what she had seen and heard of the character of Mr. Welford) with the idea that any persuasions, any arguments, any supplications of her father could induce him to act with forbearance; she was satisfied that he was just the man, like his son, to take every cowardly advantage of the power he had over them, not to persist in his hateful demands, and she therefore saw nothing but the most fearful misery before her, for it was not possible that she could suffer her father's name and liberty sacrificed, when it was in her power to save him from such a fate, even though in doing so she must forfeit her own life, and, as the wife of Everard Welford, she was thoroughly convinced that she could not possibly survive long. The very thoughts of a union with a man whom she now so thoroughly detested was almost sufficient to drive her to madness, and when she thought of her beloved Norman Rayborne, the vows they had plighted so solemnly, so earnestly together, and contrasted his character with that of his unmanly, tyrannical and brutal rival, her heart was almost ready to burst.

Many were the scalding tears of anguish she shed as she reflected on the misfortunes her parents had encountered, at least so far as they had been related to her by her father, and she looked forward to the further disclosure he had to make with the most dreadful forebodings. Again and again she humbly implored the Almighty to avert the fearful evils which were evidently impending over the heads of her and her father, and not to allow their bitter and implacable enemies to triumph over them; for without the interposition of that All Merciful Being, she saw but too plainly, that nothing could save them from the danger with which they were threatened.

She half regretted that her father had been prevented from making a disclosure of all the melancholy circumstances of his case, as it would at least have been some slight relief to her mind; but she had heard sufficient to excite her utmost alarm and terror. It was evident that her father's extreme emotion and dread of Mr. Welford and his son arose from no trifling cause, and it was not likely that he would seek to make himself more culpable than he in reality was; but still, in spite of all this, she could not entirely divest her mind of hope; she could not bring herself to believe that her unfortunate father had been guilty of all the offences at which he had hinted, and of which he had accused himself, and she trusted that his further explanation would confirm her in these ideas, and offer some extenuation for conduct which he had made to appear so guilty, and which Everard Welford had ever represented to be as perfectly heinous.

How anxiously did she await the termination of this interview, and that it might be attended with much more favourable results than she had but too much reason to fear. Several times she was half tempted to hasten to the door of the apartment in which they were, in order that she might listen to their conversation, but she could not muster courage sufficient to do so, and some instinctive power seemed to withhold her. Yet it was a great trial to her patience, and it was not without the utmost difficulty she could support it.

That her father would exert all his energies in appealing to Mr. Welford, she was well convinced, but she feared with little success, for after what her father had intimated, it seemed too clear that he had so deeply framed his plans and determinations, that he had so artfully contrived his whole guilty plot, that it was not at all likely he would be easily persuaded to abandon what he had been at so much trouble to bring about. No, upon mature deliberation she saw not the least room for hope, and she awaited the termination of the interview between her father and Mr. Welford, with the full conviction of having her worst fears confirmed.

But we must now return to the two gentlemen, and make the reader acquainted with what took place between them.

Mr. Welford on his entrance into the apartment, found his unfortunate victim seated in a chair, pale and trembling, but with a powerful effort to conquer his emotion, he arose, and attempted to stammer out some words, in which he failed, and again sinking back in his chair, he covered his face with his hands, and the heaving of his chest plainly showed the intense anguish of mind he was at that moment undergoing.

Ah, most keenly indeed did he feel the degradation of his situation, and notwithstanding all his efforts, he could not so far conquer his emotion as to meet the man whom he had so much reason to fear, and whose motives for seeking the present interview, he perfectly comprehended with firmness. He dreaded to hear him begin, and was perfectly at a loss what answer he should make him to whatever he might have to say.

It is needless to say that Mr. Welford fully remarked and understood the emotion under which he was labouring, and a smile of exultation, and secret malice passed over his features. He coolly took a seat, and remained for some moments silent, and gazing earnestly at him.

"Major Clarence," he said at length, in tones half sarcastic, "I regret to see that you have not yet entirely recovered from your recent accident, and no doubt you have felt somewhat surprised that I have not called upon you before."

Mr. Clarence looked up, and when he saw the expression of his companion's countenance, he could not help shuddering, and with the greatest difficulty faltered out,—

"I am obliged to you, Mr. Welford, for the sympathy you express for me in my misfortunes, and I trust that it will be carried out to the fullest extent, not only for my sake, but for that of one whose happiness is far more precious to me than my own existence. But I pray you excuse me at present, for I am not at all prepared for this interview."

"Pardon me, Major Clarence," returned the other, haughtily, "but I consider that you should have been prepared for it long ago. I suppose you can readily guess the business which brings me here?"

"Alas! alas, too well I know it."

"'Tis well you do, for it will save me the trouble of an explanation."

"Oh, Mr. Welford." groaned Mr. Clarence, looking up imploringly in his face; "spare me, spare my poor innocent child, I implore you, I throw myself and her on your mercy."

"Pshaw!" returned Welford impatiently, "this is sheer trifling; you know the conditions of our compact, you know the power I hold over you, and cannot avoid the consequences. This is not a time for delay, or to make fruitless appeals to my forbearance; but lest any circumstance of the past should have slipped your memory, I will take the trouble to remind you of the position in which you stand. I was your friend when you were deserted by your parents. I lent you money, I tendered you advice; and more, as a proof of my friendship, I wished to see our families at some future time united by a marriage between our children. You made a solemn vow that such should be the case if they arrived at years of maturity. Did you not do so?"

"'Tis too true, but from what motives, what real motives, let me ask you, Mr. Welford, did you exact that fatal promise. Was it not avarice, the most sordid avarice that guided you, and not from those sentiments of friendship and esteem which you would now make it appear prompted you? Although I was then placed in the most difficult circumstances, you was well aware I should be rich, and that my daughter would possess a fortune far greater than that which you could bestow upon your son."

"Indeed, so that is your opinion?" said Mr. Welford, with a bitter sneer.

"However, it matters not to me how you judge my motives; it is quite sufficient for me that you entered into the agreement, and that you must not, you dare not attempt to escape from the fulfilment of it. But I have not compled my recapitulation of facts yet, and it is necessary that your memory should be refreshed upon all those peculiar subjects by which you are placed entirely in my power."

"Oh, forbear, forbear, Welford, I have long since acknowledged my guilt, and offered every atonement in my power. Oh, why then pursue me with such miserable malice?"

"You shall hear me out. I was obliged for a time to leave the country, but before I did so, I advanced a large sum to you to supply your necessities."

"Why repeat that? Did I not afterwards repay you every farthing I had borrowed of you, with ample interest. I am indebted to you for nothing."

"You are, for your life."

Mr. Clarence groaned, and once more hid his face in his hands.

"I see," resumed Welford, evidently triumphing in the misery, the dreadful anguish he was causing in the bosom of his hapless victim; "I see that you have not the effrontery to deny that, and it is well for you that you have not. And now let me fully remind you of all your guilt."

"Oh, Welford, do not torture my ears by a repetition of that which is too fearfully impressed upon my memory."

"You rushed into acts of dissipation and extravagance," continued Welford, heeding not the supplications and the agony of Major Clarence, "you squandered in wilful waste every farthing you possessed, and then had the impudence to write to me for another loan, which I having heard of the career of vice you had been pursuing, very properly and in common justice to myself, declined to advance; and what did you then? What was the return you made me, Major Clarence, for all my disinterested acts of friendship towards you?"

"Oh, it was the madness of despair that drove me to it, and bitterly has my conscience ever since reproached me for it."

"You forged a cheque for a large sum of money in my name on my banker, and obtained the cash. I afterwards detected the crime, and could have consigned you to the gallows, but I suffered mercy to prevail, I yielded to the prayers and entreaties of yourself and your wife, and concealed your offence from every one; nay I even went so far as to admit you again to my friendship. That guilty document is still in my hands, and its production will condemn you any day. I ask you again, what is the return you have made me for all these acts of generosity. Notwithstanding the solemn compact entered into between us, you have winked at, if not actually encouraged the addresses of that beggar, Norman Rayborne, to your daughter, and now when my son comes forward to demand the hand of her to whom he is affianced, she not only scornfully rejects his suit, but insults him as well."

"Would you have me break my poor girl's heart, Welford?"

"Bah! that is mere idle twaddle."

"Ethelinde cannot love your son, and what but misery could ever attend their union?"

"Well," coolly returned Welford, "you know the alternative. Do you choose to fulfil your compact, or to be consigned to shame and punishment?"

The countenance of Major Clarence was ghastly pale as he looked up with an imploring expression of features at his remorseless interrogator.

"Welford," he gasped forth, at last, "you can never for the sake of our old friendship, and the atonement I have made you proceed to the extremes you threaten."

"You calculate too much upon my forbearance, Major Clarence," replied Mr. Welford, "which has already, been shown towards you to a far greater extent than you had any reasonable right to expect. But think you that I am a madman, or forget altogether what is due to mine own honour, and my son's future happiness as tamely to yield to the idle twaddling arguments you have put forth to evade the just fulfilment of the compact which has been entered into between us? If you do so, you will find yourself most grievously mistaken. It has become published to the world, it is a notorious theme amongst all parties that Ethelinde Clarence is my son's affianced wife, and think you that I will subject himself and me to the voice of calumny and insult, when I have it in my power to demand the consummation of all his wishes. You must deem me worse than a madman if you think that I will be guilty of any such weakness. No, Major Clarence, I come, in the absence of my son, to tell you once for all, that either your daughter becomes his wife, or less than twenty-four hours after your refusal you will find yourself the inmate of a prison on the heinous charge of forgery, and of which I hold the incontestible proofs in my possession."

"Oh, God! oh, God!" cried Mr. Clarence, beating his breast, "what a miserable, guilty wretch I am, thus to have murdered the happiness of one so fair, so dutiful, so innocent. But still I cannot believe, Mr. Welford, that you can be so entirely destitute of all feeling as to proceed to the extremities which you have threatened."

"You have heard what I have said," returned Mr. Welford, "and I now wait your answer to the question I have just put to you."

"Oh, give me, I pray, some time for consideration."

"It requires none. I should be worse than an idiot if I permitted you to tamper with me thus. You know the obligations you are under to me ; the power I possess over you ; the agreement you have signed years since, and it therefore rests to your own option whether or not you think proper to break it, and to risk the certain and degrading consequences."

"At least I implore you to hear some consideration for my poor child."

"Not at the sacrifice of all my son's future prospects," replied Welford, "at least when I have the power to prevent it. Ethelinde, your daughter, loves Norman Rayborne, does she not?"

"Alas! she has in the sincerity and innocence of her heart, acknowledged to me that she does;" replied Major Clarence.

"And you have encouraged their passion?"

"Never, never, you know that I have not."

"You never attempted to prevent their meeting, their intercourse with each other."

"True, true, I did not;" answered Mr. Clarence, "how could I thus throw a blight upon the friendship of two young and amiable beings."

"Bah!" impatiently ejaculated Mr. Welford, and a dark frown settled upon his brow, "sickening, disgusting cant, it is clear, as I before said, that in spite of the solemn, the irrevocable engagements you had entered into with me, you gave encouragement to the passion of the beggar Norman Rayborne and your daughter Ethelinde."

"No, no, I did not," returned Major Clarence ; "but he was worthy most amiable, and could I deny him my friendship when his father had been my most esteemed friend?"

"Yes, it was at once your duty to have seperated them when you knew that your daughter was bound to another and that on that one she must bestow her hand if she would save her father from being denounced to the world as a villain."

"Heaven save me," groaned Mr. Clarence, "in what a dreadful dilemma has one act of guilt placed me. What inconceivable misery has it brought upon her whose happiness is dearer to me than my very life. Mr. Welford, why will you persist in this cruel persecution? There is no sacrifice that I am not ready to make independant of that of my darling child. Command my fortune, and it is your's if you will but release me from the fearful shackles which bind us together."

"Not so, Mr. Clarence," answered Welford, with a look of scorn ; "I have sworn to carry out my plans, in spite of every consequence, and I am not so easily to be tempted to break my oath, if you are."

"I repeat to you once more, most earnestly, most impressively, that however my poor Ethelinde may regard your son as a friend, she can never view him with any more tender sentiment."

"And I repeat," said Mr. Welford, determinedly, "that she must either learn to regard him as her future husband, or consign her father to a dungeon and an ignominious fate! You know the terms on which alone you can purchase your liberty and name, and therefore, what necessity is there for me to have so often to repeat them to you ?"

Mr. Clarence gazed at him for a minute or two with the most intense anguish and despair, and then with clasped hands, he sank on his knees at his feet. It was indeed a melancholy, a pitiable sight to behold the aged and unfortunate gentleman in such a degrading position, kneeling in humble supplication before that man who was unworthy of the respect of his fellow creatures, had his real character become known. But Welford beheld it with the most inhuman exultation, and saw that the ultimate success of his diabolical plans were certain.

"Mr. Welford," cried the wretched Major, in a voice half choked with emotion, "behold me at your feet, an attitude I never before assumed to human being. For the love of Heaven, as you hope for mercy from above, I implore you to look with compassion on me and my innocent child, and to act at least with forbearance towards us."

"Rise, Major Clarence," said Mr. Welford haughtily, "although I am satisfied to see that you have not forgotten the proper deference you owe to me, I wish not to see you thus assume the character of an abject beggar."

"What is it you require of me ?"

"You ask me for forbearance,—to what extent does your supplication go ?"

Mr. Clarence again slowly arose from his knees, and for a minute or two, he felt shame and self-reproach at the humiliating position into which his agony of mind had suffered him to plunge himself, especially before one who had proved himself to be unworthy of anything but his scorn and hatred. But, alas! he soon saw the utter inutility of giving vent to those feelings, which could only bring destruction upon himself and Ethelinde, and he controlled them in the best manner he was able, while he answered :—

"I would again implore you not to urge the the fulfilment of my fatal engagement, for the present, Mr. Welford. It is necessary that Ethelinde should at least have some time to reflect upon that in which the whole of her happiness is involved, and surely your son would not think of accepting her under such circumstances."

"Be more explicit," said Mr. Welford, "this is not the time to mince matters, especially between those who understand each other so well as I believe you and I do. You seek for delay, what is the period to which you wish the fulfilment of our agreement to be procrastinated ?"

"Ethelinde is yet young, very young," replied Mr. Clarence, eagerly, "too young to think of entering into the solemn state of matrimony. Norman Rayborne has left his native country with an uncertainty that he will ever return, so that you have nothing to apprehend from him."

"Well—well !"

"Give her a respite of three years, and —"

"And do you take me for such a consummate fool," hastily interrupted Welford," as to consent to this evasion? Three years! Ha! ha! ha! the idea is in itself absurd, and could only have originated in the brain of a madman. You ought to know me better, Major Clarence, than to think I am thus to be cajoled. Three years, indeed, and in the meantime you may die, and your daughter would not then hesitate to resolutely refuse the hand of my son, since she would know that you had escaped the disgrace and punishment that such a refusal now would incur."

"Would that I were dead," sighed Mr. Clarence, "that I had died ere I had so fatally committed myself or that my unfortunate, my deeply injured child had never been born. But you will not persist in your determination, Mr. Wal ford, you cannot surely be so destitute of all reason and proper feeling as to remain entirely inexorable ?"

"You have heard my decree, and it is a useless waste of time to urge me further now."

"Say not so, I again in the most humble manner beseech you. If you will not consent to the delay I have mentioned, at least give me and my dear Ethelinde some reasonable time to reflect."

"Well," said Welford, after a pause, "since you are so urgent, and to show you that I can be forbearant, though you have not given me credit for it, I will consent to postpone the fulfilment of the contract for—for six months."

"Six months! No longer?"

"Not a day!" answered Mr. Welford, resolutely; "and let you and your daughter look well to your conduct in the meantime; for, mark me, should I observe anything in your behaviour to excite my suspicion, I will no longer delay putting my revenge into effect."

Major Clarence clasped his hands in despair, and Welford added,—

"And remember, for it is necessary you should thoroughly understand me, during that time my son must be allowed to continue his visits to Ethelinde, and she must receive him with proper respect, and listen with patience to his addresses. Moreover, I enjoin you to use your utmost efforts to promote their attachment, and to banish the image of Norman Rayborne from your daughter's mind.

"Alas! that is impossible."

"But it must be so, and you know what the consequences will be if you disobey me."

"Oh, how severe is the task you impose upon me, Welford," said Mr. Clarence, shuddering when he thought upon the probable troubles that were in store for him and his beloved Ethelinde.

"You must submit to it," said the other haughtily, "on no other conditions will I consent to the delay I have mentioned. At the expiration of six months I shall expect to see everything amicably arranged, and that Ethelinde has got rid of that perverse folly which at present holds possession of her better sense. This interview has now been protracted long enough, and I therefore bid you

farewell, once more advising you to reflect well upon what I have said, and if you value your own liberty and character, if you regard the happiness and future prospects of your daughter, to attempt not, to dare not but to act in strict obedience to my demands. There must be no trifling, no deception in the matter; you know me, and are consequently aware that if you break your word towards me, I will, at any rate, not fail to fulfil the threats I have made to you.

As Mr. Welford gave utterance to these words, without waiting for any reply from Major Clarence, he stalked from the room and abruptly quitted the mansion.

Mr. Clarence sank in his chair, and clasping his hands, for some time gave himself up entirely to the power of his emotions.

CHAPTER X.

MAJOR CLARENCE COMMUNICATES THE PARTICULARS OF THE INTERVIEW TO HIS DAUGHTER.—HER ANGUISH AND ILLNESS.

As soon as Ethelinde heard from her maid Jane, that Mr. Welford had departed from the mansion, with a trembling step and an anxious heart she left her own chamber, and proceeded to the apartment in which she had left her father. To say that she anticipated any favourable result from the interview would be wrong, for she had experienced too much of the character of Mr. Welford and his son to lead her to hope.

On entering, she found her unfortunate father in the same melancholy attitude we have described in the previous chapter. He was so absorbed in his own thoughts, that he did not notice her entrance, until she had eagerly advanced towards him, and throwing her arms around his neck called tenderly upon his name. Then he hastily raised his head, and she could see from the ghastly aspect of his countenance, and the melancholy expression of his eyes, the severe trials to which his feelings had been put at the meeting with Mr. Welford.

It was some time before either of them could find strength sufficient to utter a syllable, but at length our heroine said—

"Alas! my father, I plainly perceive from your looks, that your interview with Mr. Welford has been one of the most painful description, and that he has treated with indifference and contempt all your appeals to him for mercy and forbearance."

"It is too true, my poor child," replied her father; "but I am not disappointed. I well knew before that he was totally insensible to every feeling of pity and generosity. Oh, what a wretch have I been thus to have placed myself in the power of such a man!"

ETHELINDE FAINTING ON HEARING HER FATHER DENOUNCED AS A FORGER.

"Do not thus cruelly reproach yourself, my dear father," said Ethelinde.

"Can I do otherwise, child," returned the old man, "when I think of the misery and shame into which I have plunged you? In vain did I supplicate to him for mercy. He is inexorable, and Heaven only knows what will become of us."

"Did you entreat him to consent to a delay?"

"Oh, most urgently, most vehemently did I, my poor girl; Heaven knows I could not have pleaded more ardently had I been supplicating for my life."

"And he refused you?"

Mr. Clarence shook his head, as he replied,—

"A delay of six months is all that he would agree to; and at the termination of that period, he insists that you shall become the wife of Everard Welford, or he threatens that which he has unhappily the power to put into execution, namely, to deliver me into the hands of justice."

"Six months!" ejaculated the damsel, with a shudder of horror.

"Yes, Ethelinde; and moreover, he insists that during that time you shall receive the attentions of his son with proper respect, and banish Norman Rayborne from your memory."

"Hideous thought! Never, never can I comply with such a brutal, such an unnatural demand."

"Then, my beloved child, the fate of your miserable and guilty father is sealed, and I may as well at once resign myself to it. But to see you plunged into shame and misery, how it tortures my heart to think of that."

"Great God of Heaven, instruct me how to act!" cried Ethelinde, with a burst of anguish. "But endeavour to calm your feelings, my dear father, and relate to me all that passed at the interview between you and that bad man."

Mr. Clarence paused, and then after a violent struggle with his feelings, he complied with his daughter's request, and detailed the particulars of the conversation that had passed between him and Mr. Welford.

How poor Ethelinde shuddered as she listened to him, and frequently she could not help interrupting him to give expression to her feelings of horror and astonishment. The whole of her unfortunate father's dreadful secret was explained in that conversation; she saw at once that she must sacrifice her own happiness or consign one of the best of parents to shame; the vows she had made to Norman Rayborne must be broken; his hopes crushed for ever, and overwhelmed with the maddening reflections these facts engendered, she sank senseless in the arms of her father.

"My God! my God!" exclaimed Major Clarence, as he pressed the insensible form of his daughter to his bosom, and gazed with indescribable anguish upon her pale face, "what a wretch have I been. My Ethelinde, my darling Ethelinde, I am your murderer!"

With as much care as his agitation would permit, he placed her upon the sofa, and then rang the bell for the attendance of her maid. She came, and our heroine was removed to her chamber, while Mr. Clarence retired to his study, and gave vent to his feelings of agony in convulsive sobs and tears. Yes, Major Clarence, who had never shrunk from meeting the foe in the most dangerous positions on the battle-field, felt himself unmanned on this occasion, for the future happiness of his beloved child was sacrificed, unless Mr. Welford would relent, or he himself should brave the threats which he had held out against him.

A sudden thought darted across the mind of Mr. Clarence, and as it did so his eyes flashed with a wildness which they had never before assumed, and his bosom heaved with the most violent emotion.

"She *shall not* become the wife of Everard Welford;" he exclaimed, determinedly, "it would be monstrous to permit such a sacrifice; it would be cowardly and unnatural in me to allow such a sacrifice. In spite of the boasted triumph of the villain in whose power I have unfortunately placed myself, it can be prevented, and shall be done. Dear Ethelinde, you can better lose your father than have your young hopes blighted in this barbarous manner. Heaven pardon me for the crime, but I see no other means of rescuing you, my child."

The expression of the major's countenance, as he uttered those words was most solemn and extraordinary; it was perfectly evident that there was something more passing in his mind at that trying moment than might meet the outward gaze; he seemed fully to feel the weight of his own fearful thoughts, and kneeling down he prayed mentally to Heaven.

He started up as if inspired by a sudden impulse, and his countenance brightened; he composed his feelings, and then hastened to the chamber of his daughter, to ascertain her condition. He found her in a state of unconsciousness, attended by Mr. Charlton, who drew him aside, and in a compassionate voice, observed—

"Your daughter's mind, Major Clarence, has been overpowered by some weight of care that is more than her strength can support, and I am fearful that it will be some time before she will recover from it. I can perfectly understand the nature of it, and as your friend and personal adviser, I must prohibit the future visits of Mr. Welford or his son. Hear me, sir," he continued, as he noticed the extreme agitation of Mr. Clarence, and that he was about to make some reply, "I need no explanation from you, for it is no business of mine to inquire into the peculiar circumstances that connect you with the Welfords, but it is my professional duty to insist that your daughter should not be exposed to any excitement that, in her present state, might be productive of the most serious consequences."

"God help and pardon me," groaned Mr. Clarence, beating his breast, "would that I were dead."

"Forbear, my dear sir," returned the worthy doctor, "utter not such words."

"I am the cause of all this;" cried the major, "I am the guilty author of it all. Oh, my sweet child," he continued, stooping down over the couch and imprinting delirious kisses upon Ethelinde's pale cheeks; "to what a fate of misery has one act of crime of mine consigned me. Mr. Charlton, I know you are sincerely my friend; tell me then, I implore you, is there any immediate danger."

"The shock which this poor girl has received," replied the doctor, "is a most serious one, and it may be some time before she recovers from it; but compose yourself, Mr. Clarence, and depend upon it that I will exert all my skill towards ensuring her restoration. There is one thing I would advise, for I think it may tend towards her convalescence."

"Oh, name it, my dear, good sir," ejaculated the major eagerly, "I will be guided entirely by your advice."

"Mrs. Rayborne and her amiable daughter are her favourite companions," replied Mr. Charlton, "and I recommend that they should be requested to visit her as frequently as possibly."

"Most duly do I appreciate the virtues and the friendship of those two estimable ladies," sighed Mr. Clarence, "but alas!—"

"I know what you would say, sir," interrupted the doctor, "and will make it my business, with your permission, to call on Mr. Welford and his son, to arrange the business. They cannot be blind to the necessity of complying with my request, and if they are, I shall consider it my duty, knowing the situation of this poor girl, to insist upon it, so do not suffer this to trouble you."

Mr. Clarence pressed his hand, but could not at the moment return any answer. Again we approached the bedside of his daughter, and taking her hand in his own, he looked with feelings of the most intense emotion in her face. At that moment she recovered to sensibility, and opening her beauteous eyes, fixed them, with a vacant expression, upon her father.

"'Tis me, my love, my Ethelinde," he exclaimed; "do you not know me?"

"No, no, I know you not," returned the poor girl, wildly; "and yet methinks I do now,—oh, yes, you are the father of him who would supplant Norman Rayborne in my heart's warm love; but your arts shall not prevail; no, no, I have pledged my word to him to whom my whole soul is devoted, and who shall compel me to break that vow made in the sight of Heaven? Under the seventh oak tree in the dale!—oh yes, I remember, I remember!"

"My God! my God!" exclaimed the distracted father, "her senses have left her."

"Oh, it will be a jovial wedding," continued the poor girl, in the same wild strain, and smiles, which from their unnatural character were quite agonizing to look upon; "it will be a jovial wedding, and how delighted Everard Welford and his father will be to witness it. They said that Everard was my own dear Norman's rival, that he sought my love, and that there was a certain fatal vow which compelled me to become his bride, or to consign my father to the gallows. Ha! ha! ha! How ridiculous! how absurd!"

And then she looked more wildly and vacantly around the room, and laughed hysterically.

Oh, what tortures at that moment distracted the brain of Major Clarence! He knelt by the side of Ethelinde's bed, and with clasped hands called frantically upon her name, and supplicated her forgiveness; but she fixed the vacant stare of madness upon him, and it was evident she knew him not.

"Gracious Heaven!" he cried, striking his forehead, "what a scene is this for a father's feelings to have to endure! Oh Welford, much as I have sinned against you, how much have you to answer for! would that I were dead!"

"Mr. Clarence," said Mr. Charlton, "let me beg of you not to give way to these violent paroxysms, and to retire. Alarming as the situation of your daughter may appear to be, I have no doubt that she will soon recover, and that these painful symptoms will abate. But certainly your presence will only tend to retard her recovery and not to promote it. I will, with your leave, despatch a messenger to Mrs. Rayborne, requesting her attendance."

"You are right, sir, you are right," said Mr. Clarence in a melancholy tone of voice, and pressing the worthy doctor's hand, "I must, I will be guided by you in everything. God help me, God preserve me, I am a poor, weak, wretched being."

As he spoke, he tottered towards the bedside of his daughter once more, and throwing his arms around her neck, kissed her vehemently, whilst his tears flowed fast upon her cheeks. She offered no resistance to his embraces, but she still stared at him vacantly, and it was evident that she was quite unconscious who he was. Mr. Charlton rang the bell and when the servant answered the summons, he desired that she would see her master to his own apartments, and then attend upon him again in a few minutes."

The major turned one sad look upon his suffering daughter, and then sighing deeply, but without uttering another word, he solemnly walked from the chamber, followed by the servant. On entering his own apartment, he desired to be alone, and throwing himself on his knees, covered his face with his hands, and remained for some time buried in a state of almost utter unconsciousness of what was passing.

Mr. Charlton dispatched a letter to Mrs. Rayborne, informing her of all that had taken place, and requesting her attendance, and in a short time that excellent woman and the lovely Kate, her daughter, arrived, and entered the chamber of the suffering girl. The worthy doctor also forwarded a letter to Mr. Welford, in which, without any exaggeration, he described the painful effects of his interview with Major Clarence, and respectfully, but urgently desired that neither he nor his son would attempt to resort to any measures which might increase the malady under which the poor girl suffered, and be productive of the most fatal consequences.

Mr. Welford and his son received the intelligence with the greatest confusion and alarm. Everard, in particular, stamped and raved like a madman.

"Ethelinde will be lost to me after all," he ejaculated. "Fate frowns upon me; curses light upon i , are there no means of removing these obstacles to my suit?"

"None at present," replied his father, "common decency prevents our obtruding ourselves at the mansion of Major Clarence during the illness of Ethelinde. But do not despair; she will recover, Norman Rayborne is far away; Clarence is completly in our power, and nothing whatever can ultimately prevent the success of our plans."

Everard endeavoured to be content, but powerful doubts and fears distracted his mind, and he was continually sending messages to the house of Mr. Clarence to inquire after the progress of our heroine, and expressed the deepest sympathy in her illness. To hear, however, that the mother and sister of his rival were in constant attendance upon her, was a source of the greatest chagrin to him, and he could scarcely contain himself within the bounds of reason.

With the most assiduous care did Mrs. Rayborne and her daughter watch by the couch of the fair invalid, and administer all that they could to the relief of her and her disconsolate father, who was almost reduced to a state of frenzy; but all that night and the following day the poor girl continued in the same state of unconsciousness, and raved in the most wild and incoherent manner. How bitterly it wrung the hearts of Mrs. Rayborne and Kate to hear the tender allusions which she made to Norman. It was a severe trial to all parties, but none felt it more keenly than the parent of the sufferer.

He reproached himself as being the author of it all, and at times he was driven to such a pitch of madness and despair as almost to attempt to commit suicide.

Towards the evening of the following day, however, a favourable change came over our heroine; she was awakened to sensibility, and knew those about her. With what affection did her father embrace her, and implore her to forgive him for the sufferings which his own early misconduct, and the rash vow he had made, had caused her.

"Oh, forbear! forbear! my dear father!" she exclaimed, "if you would not drive me into the same state of madness from which I have just recovered. Heaven forbid that I should accuse you of that which my heart assures me you are not guilty of. You have been made the victim of villany, and heaven will yet thwart it in its diabolical designs."

"My sweet girl," returned her father, "I deserve not this. Oh—but I will say no more, God be thanked for having so far restored you, and may He in his infinite mercy avert all the other evils by which you are at present threatened. How much do we owe to the kindness of these our two excellent friends, Mrs. Rayborne and her daughter."

"Mention it not, my dear sir," said Mrs. Rayborne, "were Ethelinde my own child, or the sister of my Kate, we could not love her better than we do, or feel a greater anxiety in her welfare."

Sweetly our heroine smiled upon them, and extended her hands to them, which they pressed affectionately to their lips, and the scene became one of the most interesting and impressive description.

The favourable change that had taken place in Ethelinde continued, but still neither Kate nor her mother could be prevailed upon to leave her for a moment, and they attended to all her wants with the most anxious care. But there were times when it required all their exertions to calm her feelings or to banish the recollection of the interview that had taken place between her father and Mr. Welford, and in which had been disclosed the whole of the fearful secret she had long been so anxious to know. She saw herself and her father, by it, placed entirely at the mercy of Welford and his son, and she could not help shuddering with a sensation of the most unconquerable horror at the prospect of the dangers by which she was still threatened.

Mr. Clarence was at length persuaded to leave the chamber of his daughter, and when he had reached his own apartment, he again threw himself upon his knees, and returned his thanks to the Supreme Being, for her having been so far recovered. But still the most dark, and gloomy, and torturing thoughts continued to harass his mind; and although he tried his utmost to do so, he could not divest his mind of them.

"By Heaven! by all my hopes!" he cried, "never will I sacrifice my beloved child to the man she loathes and despises, let whatever may be the consequences. What better than a murderer should I be were I to do so?—I have been to blame, oh, much to blame, not to have shown more resolution ere this. But I will be so no longer. No, I will put my trust in the mercy of Providence who knows my compunction and the years of suffering and remorse I have experienced, for the faults which in my youth I committed, and will not forsake me or my poor child in this the hour of our need."

He felt more calm and confident after this, and endeavoured to look forward to the future with renewed hope.

Mr. Welford and his son were delighted when they heard of the favourable change that had taken place in our heroine, and that she was likely speedily to recover, and notwithstanding the excitement which he knew it must naturally cause in the mind of the poor girl, Everard could scarcely be prevailed upon from again visiting the mansion of Mr. Clarence; however, Dr. Charlton made it his business according to promise, to call upon him and his father, and so forcibly urged upon him and his father the impropriety and the danger of their intruding themselves upon Ethelinde and her father for the present, that they were forced, though reluctantly, to yield, and sent a message to the major and his daughter, couched in language of sympathy, and congratulation on the prospect of the latter's recovery, but which, as might have been expected, was not calculated to deceive either of them, but was more likely to excite disgust and alarm in their breasts.

CHAPTER XI.

REMARKABLE CHANGES. — FORTUNE SMILES UPON MRS. RAYBORNE.—THE EXPECTED RETURN.—THE ILLNESS AND DEATH OF MR. WELFORD.

IN the course of three weeks, Ethelinde was so far recovered as to be able to leave her chamber, and to take gentle airings, accompanied by her father and Mrs. Rayborne, and her daughter. But still great was the weight of care which pressed upon her mind, and in vain she sought to forget the interview between her father and Mr. Welford. In six months she must either consent to become the wife of the detested Everard, or expose her father to a fate from which her very soul recoiled with horror. Would, she reflected, that it had pleased Heaven to take her to itself when she was in that happy state of unconsciousness, there would then have been an end to her troubles, and surely their bitter enemies would then have ceased to persecute her poor father.

But what Ethelinde now most dreaded was a visit from Everard Welford. She knew not how she should ever find sufficient fortitude to meet him and certainly she could never comply with the demands of his father, merely, that she should receive his odious advances with favour and respect.

The time so much dreaded at length arrived. Everard sent word that he should do himself the honour and the pleasure of visiting her on the following day, and hoped that she would be prepared to receive him in a becoming manner. Need we attempt to describe the agony of the poor girl's feelings, or that of her father on receiving this message, so painful and unwelcome? We are certain we need not, but they knew it would be useless to attempt to excuse themselves, for Everard was determined, and any opposition on their part might only provoke him to proceed to extremities, and might be productive of the most fatal consequences.

The morning came, and punctual to the hour Everard Welford arrived. He met our heroine with much apparent respect, and congratulated her on her recovery. She turned ghastly pale at the sight of him, and for some minutes she was so overpowered by her feelings that she could not repeat a syllable, but averted her face, fearful of raising her eyes towards him. When she did partly recover herself, she scarcely knew how she replied to him, but at length she burst into tears, and clasping her fair hands together, implored him to take pity on her.

"I know," she, continued, "that I and my unfortunate father are in your power; I know all the dreadful truth; but surely you cannot be lost to all feeling, after the sincere penitence and remorse he has expressed, and the ample atonement he has offered to make, to persist in your present vindictive feelings towards him, and to extend that feeling to me."

"I would bestow upon you my love, my hand, my fortune, fair Ethelinde," answered Everard, "you are plighted to me by a solemn vow, and think not that I will yield my right to Norman Rayborne. But why remain obdurate? What is there so transcendent in the pretensions of Norman Rayborne, that none other but he can find a place in your affections?"

"Everard Welford," replied Ethelinde firmly, "I have before told you that even though it be not my fate to become the wife of Norman Raybone to whom my vows were plighted, you can never possess my love. Formerly I looked upon you with esteem, but for for some time past, you have taken great pains to forfeit all claim to that."

Everard bit his lips, and in vain endeavoured to conceal his vexation.

"Remonstrances or arguments, proud beauty, I see are entirely lost upon you," he said at last; "but mark my words; love me, or love me not, at the time appointed, nothing shall prevent you from becoming my wife, unless indeed you prefer consigning your father to a felon's fate."

"Cruel man," ejaculated our heroine, with a shudder of disgust, "will nothing move you to a sense of pity or justice."

"Treat not my sentiments with scorn," replied Everard, "and you shall find me all that woman can desire in man."

"Never, never; my heart revolts at the idea," said Ethelinde, turning from him, and hiding her blushing face in her handkerchief.

"Then you know the consequences;" cried Everard, with an air of determination; "farewell; I shall yet find the way to break this obstinate spirit, or I am much mistaken."

Ethelinde might have answered that he would find the way to break her heart first, but much to her relief he abruptly left the room, and quitted the house.

Almost every day was our heroine annoyed by the visits of Everard Welford, and it was wonderful how she supported them with the fortitude she did, and great was the agony which her father endured to behold the insult and suffering to which she was exposed, and from which he had no power of extricating her. Yes, there was one way, and he often anticipated it, but the means were dreadful, and he feared that they would only plunge her into still greater misery, if possible, than if she were to become the wife of the hated Everard Welford.

Several weeks passed away without anything particular occurring; Everard continued to pay his addresses to Ethelinde, but with no better success than before, and he anxiously looked forward to the expiration of the time, when he had determined to make her his bride; but notwithstanding the present unpromising state of affairs, Ethelinde could not help at times entertaining a hope that something would occur to release her and her father from the power of their enemies, and it was that hope which sustained her under so many severe trials.

It was a matter of the greatest vexation and jealousy to Mr. Welford and his son to see the intimacy which was kept up between Mrs. Rayborne, Major Clarence, and Ethelinde; she and her daughter were almost daily visitors at the mansion, and indeed our heroine's principal consolation was in their society. Could she banish her beloved Norman from her memory, could she forget the solemn promise she had made to him in the dell? Oh, no; that was utterly impossible. Norman Rayborne was the constant object of her thoughts, both waking and sleeping, and fervently she prayed that Heaven would guard him from every danger in a foreign land, that Providence would even before the expected time restore him to his friends, and that something would yet occur to defeat the plans of Everard Welford, and join them together in the indissoluble bonds of wedlock.

And now a great and joyous change took place in the affairs of Mrs. Rayborne, which rendered it likely that those hopes would be realized; by the death of a distant relation, Mrs. Rayborne, Kate, and Norman, each came into the possession of large estates. Nothing could exceed the joy of our heroine at this occurrence, or the chagrin and jealousy of Everard Welford and his father, who now found the family they so thoroughly hated placed in much more affluent circumstances than themselves, and they could not but apprehend that the circumstance would present some fresh obstacle to the gratification of their wishes, particularly as Mrs. Rayborne despatched a letter, by the first vessel that sailed to her son, making him acquainted with their good fortune, and desiring him to return home immediately; but still Everard knew that it was impossible he could arrive in England before the time fixed upon for his union with the lovely Ethelinde, and therefore, what had he to fear? Had he known the thoughts which were passing in her mind, he would have seen that he had everything to dread.

With the deepest anxiety did Ethelinde look forward to the return of her lover, and she was fully resolved that no earthly power should compel her to become the bride of Everard until that event took place. Major Clarence, although he rejoiced equally with his daughter in the good fortune of Mrs. Rayborne and her offspring, could not but anticipate the return of Norman with feelings of dread, for he could expect no mercy from his implacable enemies, and he must either consign his beloved child to a fate of misery, or be himself condemned to the world as a criminal, and probably be turned over to the hands of his country. Again most bitterly did he reproach himself for the errors of his former life, and deeply did he regret that fatal vow, by which he had sacrificed the future happiness of his only child.

But another event was about to take place to strengthen the hopes of Ethelinde, and to retard, if not ultimately to prevent, the gratification of the wishes of Everard Welford.

The health of Mr. Welford had long been declining, and at length he became so seriously bad, that for several days his life was despaired of. When his strength was sufficiently restored, his medical advisers considered it absolutely necessary that he should be removed to some more genial climate in order to the complete restoration of his health, and of course Everard was compelled to attend on him. We need not attempt to describe his vexation at this circumstance, for to separate himself even for the shortest period from Ethelinde was most vexatious to him, and it was now quite uncertain when his father's health would permit him to return. Before he departed, however, he had a parting interview with our heroine and her father, in which he renewed his importunities with more vehemence than ever, and warned them to remember the time appointed for the union, and at their peril to attempt to deceive him.

Ethelinde on this occasion heard him with perfect indifference, for her heart was inspired with hope, and Everard after an interview of about an hour, left the house, and the next morning he and his father departed on their journey, much to the relief of all those so deeply interested.

Three more weeks elapsed, when they received news of Mr. Welford's death, who had suffered a relapse almost immediately on his arrival at the place of his distination, and which completely baffled all the skill of his medical attendants.

This event aroused Major Clarence from the most abject despair to hope. The only witness of his offence was no more, and the power of Everard Welford was therefore no longer to be dreaded. He might proclaim his guilt to the world, but in the absence of proof, and high as his character stood in the estimation of all, who would believe it? At any rate he was determined to brave everything rather than sacrifice Ethelinde to one so unworthy of her, and whom she could not but hate and despise.

He lost no time in making our heroine acquainted with his resolution, and she received the intelligence with the most unfeigned feelings of joy, and now indeed looked forward to the return of Norman Rayborne with the most exquisite feelings of transport.

The remains of Mr. Welford were removed to England, Everard feeling much greater regret in the change which had come over his prospects than at the death of his father; he had no doubt that Mr. Clarence would take advantage of it to set his threats at defiance, especially as Mr. Welford had neglected to inform him where the forged document was concealed, and he had in vain searched for it since his return to England. He, however, immediately after the interment of his father sought an interview with Major Clarence and his daughter, and renewed his suit with the same degree of confidence he had before assumed; he was not surprised at the reception he met with.

"Everard Welford, you have before frequently heard from my lips and those of Ethelinde that she cannot love you," said Mr. Clarence, "in spite of which you have persisted in your hateful vows, and held out the most cowardly and brutal threats, in order to intimidate me into a compliance with your wishes; but now hear me, while I declare to you my determination to set you at defiance, and that no person on earth shall compel me to sacrifice the happiness of one who is far more precious than my own life."

"So this is your determination, is it, Major Clarence?" said Everard with a bitter scowl.

"That is my determination;" answered Mr. Clarence, firmly.

"Beware, sir! do you not know the danger into which you will plunge yourself by such a determination?"

"I tell you again," replied Mr. Clarence, "that I am no longer to be intimidated."

"Is it not in my power to proclaim you to the world as a forger?" demanded Everard.

"I know it, and you are at liberty to do so if you think proper. I can better endure the censure of the world than consign my child to misery."

"Have you then forgotten your vow?"

"No · but no vow exacted under

such circumstances can be binding in the sight of Heaven."

"By Heaven, this is more than I can tamely endure!" said Everard, stamping his foot, fiercely. "Major Clarence, you had better not decide too harshly. I will allow you a few days to reflect upon what I have said, and then ——"

"I require no time to deliberate," interrupted Major Clarence, determinedly, "my mind is made up already."

"Then by my soul, both you and Ethelinde shall have cause to repent it," cried Everard; "you think that by the death of my father, my power is at an

MR. CLARENCE ACCOMPANIED BY HIS DAUGHTER ON HIS RECOVERY.

end, but you will find yourself most grievously mistaken."

"I defy your power, as you are pleased to call it;" said Major Clarence, scornfully.

"I will have a terrible revenge for this insult."

"And think you that I am to be alarmed by your empty threats? I desire you to leave my house, and I will hold no further intercourse with you."

"But you shall, Major Clarence," returned Everard, "and much to your disappointment and confusion. Mark me, Ethelinde Clarence shall never become the wife of Norman Rayborne.'

As he said this, he frowned fearfully upon the major, and abruptly quitted the house. Ethelinde threw herself in her father's arms when he was gone, and wept mingled tears of gratitude and joy.

"But oh, my father," ejaculated the lovely damsel, "but should he put his threats into execution."

"Heed them not my dear child," replied her father, "they are merely the wild ebullitions of a disappointed villain."

"But he will denounce you to the world."

"And let him do so, I heed it not now ; you know the whole truth, and I can better meet the world's scandal and reproach, than suffer you to become the wife of one who is unworthy the name of a man."

Ethelinde threw herself on the bosom of her father ; her emotions were far too powerful for utterance. Of what a dreadful weight of care was her mind now relieved; her father had determinedly, peremptorily rejected the hateful suit of Everard Welford, and she might now indeed look forward to the return of Norman Rayborne with the brightest hopes.

CHAPTER XII.

THE MELANCHOLY NEWS.—SUPPOSED DEATH OF NORMAN RAYBORNE.—THE MEETING AT THE SEVENTH TREE IN THE DELL.—THE RUFFIAN, THE SURPRISE, THE ENCOUNTER.

GREAT was the rage of Everard Welford on leaving Major Clarence and his daughter, although the reception he had met with from them was no more than he had expected, after the death of his father. Notwithstanding the threats of vengeance he had held out, he knew he was powerless, and the return of Norman Rayborne to England, would prove at once the annihilation of his hopes. He determined to try what effect a more humble and gentle tone would have upon Ethelinde and her father, and accordingly in a day or two afterwards sent a letter to them, in which he apologized for the intemperate language he had made use of at their last meeting, and earnestly supplicated another interview, that he might explain. To this, Mr. Clarence returned a cold and laconic reply, in which he merely said, that he must beg leave to decline all future correspondence with him. On the receipt of this, Everard was furious, and vowed all kinds of revenge; for days he wandered near the mansion of Mr. Clarence with no settled purpose, unless it was the hope of encountering Ethelinde, but disappointed, he returned home, and a few days afterwards Ethelinde and her father were gratified to learn that he had left his residence, and had informed his servants that it was quite uncertain when he would return.

Inspired with hope, the cheerfulness of Ethelinde was restored to her, and she counted the days and hours until the time when her lover might be expected to return, with the greatest anxiety and impatience. At length a merchant vessel arrived at the port of Plymouth, and Mrs. Rayborne and Ethelinde received letters from Norman, in which he breathed the joyous sentiments of his heart, at the prospect of so soon beholding them, and informed them, that as he would be enabled to settle his arrangements in two or three days, he should return to his native land in the next homeward bound ship, the Dart, and if the voyage proved a favourable one, they might shortly expect to behold him again.

Great was now the joy of all interested ; our heroine and Mrs. Rayborne and Kate were seldom apart, and they could talk of nothing else but the joy of meeting with the noble youth from whom they had been so long separated, and many were the preparations made to receive him. As for Everard Welford, they seldom allowed him to enter their thoughts. But alas ! their joyous anticipations were doomed to receive another and a dreadful shock.

Six weeks after the receipt of Norman's letter, news reached England of the wreck of the "Dart," with the total loss of every soul on board ? Oh, what a terrible blow was this to them all ! Mrs. Rayborne and her daughter were inconsolable, and such was the effect that the fatal intelligence had upon poor Ethelinde that her senses left her; she was confined to her bed, and for several weeks she remained in so dangerous and precarious a state, that her life was despaired of.

At length, however, youth and a naturally strong constitution triumphed, and our heroine was enabled to leave her chamber; but how melancholy it was to see the sufferings she endured, and how vain it was to endeavour to impart consolation to her.

It was some time before Mrs. Rayborne and Kate could at all recover from the dreadful shock which the melancholy intelligence of the untimely fate of Norman had given them, and they then tried by all the means in their power to impart consolation to Ethelinde, which was a still more difficult undertaking.

Everard Welford, in his retreat, received almost daily intelligence, from agents he had employed, of all that took place at home, and he prepared his plans accordingly; but when he read in the paper the account of the loss of the Dart, with all hands on board, his exultation exceeded all bounds, and he determined at once to return home, and as soon as common decency would permit, to renew his addresses to Ethelinde; and with this intention he returned to his former abode.

It caused little or no excitement in the minds of Major Clarence or our heroine, when they heard of the return of Everard Welford, for they were equally determined, if he had the boldness, after his last interview with them, and the threats he had then held out, to again advance his suit, to treat him with the contempt which he deserved, and to set him at defiance; and therefore, when he did make bold enough to request an interview with Mr. Clarence, the reception he met with may be easily imagined, though at the same time it was a bitter disappointment to his hopes, and a sad outrage upon his personal vanity. He left the mansion, swearing the deepest vengeance.

Three more weeks elapsed; they were melancholy weeks to poor Ethelinde, the only consolation she could find being in the society of Mrs. Rayborne and her daughter, and in dwelling upon the virtues of her supposed departed lover. One beautiful afternoon, Major Clarence feeling rather indisposed, Ethelinde walked alone to the residence of Mrs. Rayborne, and after passing some time there in conversation, she left, desiring particularly to be allowed to return home unattended, as the night was remarkably fine, and she wished to commune with her own thoughts.

Many where the favourite places so dear to her and Norman Rayborne, that she visited, prior to her returning home, and at length she reached the dell. The moon was shining brilliantly, and Ethelinde sat on the trunk of a fallen tree, and could not restrain her tears.

While she was thus occupied, totally regardless of the time, she was suddenly aroused by the pressure of a hand upon her shoulder, and starting up, and looking round, what was her confusion and alarm at beholding Everard Welford? Her first impulse was to fly, but Everard grasped her wrist, with an air of determination, and detained her.

"Well met, sweet Ethelinde," he ejaculated, "Heaven knows how anxiously I have been watching for the opportunity which is now afforded me."

"Release me, man," commanded Ethelinde proudly, "how dare you seek to obtrude yourself upon my presence after what has taken place? Begone I say, and suffer me to return home unmolested. You will do so, if you have but one spark of manhood left within you."

"Nay think not," cried Everard, "that I am the weak fool to be easily defeated in my designs. You shall be mine, though all the world should seek to oppose my wishes."

"Help! help!" screamed Ethelinde struggling violently to rescue herself from his grasp.

Finding this to be the case, he applied a whistle to his lips, and blowing it shrilly, four other ruffians rushed from the clump of trees where they had been concealed, and surrounded our hapless heroine, ready to perform their villainous master's bidding.

"Quick! quick! away with her," commanded Everard, "you know your instructions."

"Your cries are useless!" continued Everard Welford, triumphantly, "there is no one here to help you, you are, now completely in my power."

"Liar! villain!—Cowardly knave!" shouted a loud voice, and in a moment Everard was felled insensible to the earth, by a desperate blow on the head from a stout bludgeon, and the ruffians found themselves fiercely attacked by half-a-dozen men in seamen's clothes, and were glad to take to flight as fast as their legs could carry them.

"My Ethelinde, my sweet Ethelinde! my love, my affianced bride!" exclaimed the individual who had felled the villain Everard to the earth. At the sound of the well-known voice, our heroine looked up, and uttering a cry of mingled astonishment and indescribable transport, she sunk insensible in his arms! It was Norman Rayborne!

*   *   *   *

Yes, Norman Rayborne was the only one who had been saved out of the unfortunate crew of the Dart, and being picked up by a vessel which was on her passage to England, fortunately reached the old trysting place, accompanied by some of his messmates, at the very moment when his beloved Ethelinde was placed in so much danger. Thinking to afford Ethelinde, his mother, and Kate an agreeable surprise, Norman had foolishly neglected to write as soon as he arrived in England, to inform them of his safety.

Turning to the seamen, he said,—

"Some of you convey that senseless wretch to the hall yonder, and let one of you depart to the residence of Major Clarence, which you will find a short distance from hence, and inform him of what has taken place, and that he will find me and his daughter at the house of my mother!"

The seamen hastened to fulfil their instructions, and Norman Rayborne raising the insensible form of his loves in his arms, hurried with her toward that home from which he had been so long separated, his heart overflowing with feelings of transport.

CHAPTER XII.

CONCLUSION.

It would be a matter of utter impossibility for us to describe as it ought to be, the scene which took place between all parties when they met, and our heroine recovered her senses. The sudden surprise was almost too much for them, and Norman regretted that he had not prepared them for it; but at length they recovered themselves, and the most unbounded happiness took possession of their bosoms. Norman was briefly made acquainted with the death of Mr. Welford, and all that had taken place since he had been away, and nothing could exceed the indignation he felt at the persecution to which our heroine and her father had been exposed.

"But my Ethelinde has ever remained faithful to me, nothwithstanding the fearful perils by which she has been surrounded," ejaculated Norman; "she has never forgotten the words that passed between us on the memorable night of our parting in the dell; and now that it has pleased Providence to restore me to my home, and to recruit my fortune, I trust that Major Clarence will deign to smile upon our love, and no longer refuse to sanction our union."

Mr. Clarence, who was deeply affected, joined their hands, and in a voice of emotion replied—

"Bless you, bless you, my children, for such I now consider you both to be. My heart always sanctioned your virtuous love, for I knew you both to be worthy of each other; but I was bound by a fatal vow which will be explained to you hereafter. Take her, Norman, she is your's, and may Almighty God shower down every blessing upon your union."

*   *   *   *   *

Three months after the return of Norman Rayborne to his native land, the happiness of himself and Ethelinde was complete, and great was the rejoicing that took place in the neighbourhood on the occasion of their nuptials.

All the bliss that can fall to the lot of mortals attended their union, and Major Clarence lived many years afterwards to behold them surrounded by a numerous progeny.

And Kate Rayborne, too, met the reward to which her numerous virtues entitled her, in becoming the happy wife of an excellent and wealthy man.

Everard Welford was confined by a long illness, which had a salutary effect upon his mind; and his future conduct was such as to atone in great measure for his past enormities.

THE END.